Cemetery Whites

Connie Knight

Black Rose Writing
www.blackrosewriting.com

© 2011 by Connie Knight

All rights reserved. No part of this book may be reproduced, stored in a retrieval system or transmitted in any form or by any means without the prior written permission of the publishers, except by a reviewer who may quote brief passages in a review to be printed in a newspaper, magazine or journal.

The final approval for this literary material is granted by the author.

First printing

All characters appearing in this work are fictitious. Any resemblance to real persons, living or dead, is purely coincidental.

ISBN: 978-1-61296-013-5

PUBLISHED BY BLACK ROSE WRITING

www.blackrosewriting.com

Printed in the United States of America

Cemetery Whites is printed in Adobe Hebrew

*This book is lovingly dedicated
to my family in Texas—
Hunters, Griffins, Tennilles, and Knights and more.*

*Probably the most common bearded iris grown in the South
is Iris x albicans, better known as "Cemetery Whites."
They are a naturally sterile hybrid and are extremely hardy,
often marking abandoned homesites and old cemeteries,
where for several weeks each spring they command
the attention of all passersby.*

*— William C. Welch and Greg Grant,
"The Southern Heirloom Garden"*

CHAPTER ONE
Tuesday, March 16, 2010

An ancient Oldsmobile chugged down the dry dirt road, raising a red dust cloud. The driver, an elderly woman with wispy gray hair gathered into a knot at the nape of her neck, wore a loose-fitting cotton flannel dress and a long cardigan sweater. She shared the front seat with a dapper-looking middle-aged black man, dressed in khaki slacks and a white polo shirt. His tweed jacket and a large leather briefcase occupied floor space under his feet. In the back seat rode the driver's thirty-three-year-old grandson, wearing blue jeans and a red T-shirt that showed off his muscles. His curly blond hair escaped from the edges of his baseball cap, and a denim jacket draped across his shoulders.

The driver, Henrietta Hargrove Harrell, knew her way around the dirt roads of DeWitt County. She had lived there her entire eighty-five years. Someone he knew in San Antonio had told that to Professor Thomas Harrison, so on his trip to Yorktown, he located her and knocked on her door. He introduced himself, gave her his card, and asked her to drive him to the Hargrove Family Cemetery. Seeing the graveyard would fit into some historical research of his, he said.

"I'd just ask you for directions, but I know from past attempts that it's hard to find your way around these country roads. I'm afraid I couldn't manage it. I'd drive around in circles all day."

Henrietta—Great-Aunt Hettie to the Hargrove clan—had looked at him with measuring eyes then nodded her head in agreement. She would pick him up at his motel at eight o'clock

Tuesday morning.

But just in case—just in case—she brought Donny Harrell along in the back seat, and a Colt .45 in her purse. Already loaded and ready to go if needed.

Driving along, there was little conversation among the three. Hettie concentrated on driving, Donny dozed in the back seat, and Professor Harrison paid an occasional compliment to the early wildflowers blooming along the road. It was the middle of March, his spring break from teaching at San Antonio State University. He felt optimistic about his project of the day.

None of them noticed the little gray car that followed them. The red dust cloud behind the Oldsmobile obscured it. When Hettie pulled up next to the chain-link fence surrounding the Hargrove Family Cemetery, the gray car, far in the rear, slowed almost to a stop. Then, near the far edge of the cemetery, a clump of brush on the edge of the road offered a place to park. To park and hide. The driver pulled in and switched the engine off. Through the brush, he could glimpse Hettie, Donny, and Professor Harrison getting out of the car. Harrison wore his jacket and carried his briefcase along.

Hettie opened the gate of the chain-link fence and led the way in. She turned to Thomas Harrison. "Now which graves did you want to see?"

"The old section," he said. "Some of the oldest graves are those of Thomas Watson Hargrove and his wife, Elizabeth Dennison. Settlers in the DeWitt Colony of 1825, isn't that right? He'd be your great-grandfather, wouldn't he? The ancestor of many children in this area today, and of some who have moved on to other counties, other cities."

"That's right." Hettie led the way through the large array of tombstones. Stone paths wound around clusters of shrubs and small trees. The path finally led to a group of old graves with small headstones crusted with lichens. The names and dates on them were hard to read.

Cemetery Whites

Hettie pointed to two stones near a live oak tree. A large patch of white irises, known as Cemetery Whites, were in bloom at the foot of the grave sites.

"Are these the ones you want to see?"

"Yes, yes, yes!" Gleefully, Professor Harrison placed his thick briefcase on the ground, unzipped it, and removed something from it. Zipped it back up. Then he unfolded what he had removed.

It was a tri-fold camping shovel. As Hettie and Donny watched, Professor Harrison unfolded the shovel, clamped the pieces together, and began to dig at the foot of Thomas Hargrove's grave.

Hettie and Donny were astonished, but they weren't the only ones watching. The driver of the gray car had crept closer, to see the group better. He could hear what they said.

"What are you doing?" Hettie cried. "You can't dig up my great-grandfather's grave. Stop this minute! I'm telling you to stop!"

Professor Harrison looked at her in anger. "I've been waiting for this for years. It's nothing that will hurt you, but it's important to me. Just leave me alone; it won't take long." He went back to work with his shovel.

"Stop, I say!" Hettie reached into her purse and pulled out her gun. She pointed it at Professor Harrison.

He laughed in derision and raised his shovel to knock the gun out of her hands. Donny stepped forward and reached for the shovel, but he bumped into Hettie and knocked her down. Her gun went off. Professor Harrison fell backwards, landing on the ground. A blotch of red blood soaked the front of his polo shirt and spread rapidly.

"Grandma, are you all right?" Donny reached out to Hettie and helped her get up from the ground. He picked up her gun and put it back in her purse.

Hettie stood up shakily. No broken bones. She looked at Thomas Harrison, only a few feet away. Blood gushed from his chest, and his eyes were open and blank.

"He's dead. Oh, Donny, he's dead."

"We've got to go, Grandma. We've got to get out of here." Donny took Hettie's hand and pulled her down the stone path, through the gate, into the Oldsmobile's passenger seat. Donny took the driver's seat, grabbed the keys from Hettie's purse, and gunned the old car down the road. At the next intersection, he turned left, and headed down a circular road that led back home.

He looked at Hettie. "Are you all right now?"

Her face was pale, her heart pounding. She whispered, "I'm okay." Then she added, "Let's get home. When we're there, we'll have to figure out what to do."

"You'll come up with something, Grandma. You always do."

"Not for things like this."

They barreled on home.

At the cemetery, someone else stepped up to Professor Harrison, who lay sprawled in the Cemetery Whites iris patch. The shovel was still in Harrison's hand. His own gun was still in the hand of the observer.

"Well, she didn't mean to hurt you and neither did I," the observer told the professor. "You asked for it, though. You should have shared with me."

He put his gun back in the pocket of his corduroy jacket, picked up Professor Harrison's zipped-up briefcase, and judged its weight.

"There must be a lot of paperwork in here," he said to the corpse. "Well, I'm not sticking around to look it over. I'll take it with me. But I'll be back again—when you're gone."

He turned his back on Harrison and walked slowly back to the gray car.

Cemetery Whites

CHAPTER TWO

It was almost ten o'clock in the morning in Yorktown, Texas. I looked out the window of my little study, then at the clock on the wall. I clicked PRINT on the computer I'd brought from Houston to Yorktown. Out rolled pages of family tree diagrams. While they accumulated, I watched the birds at the cluster of feeders in the side yard, then I gathered my purse, keys, folders, and DeWitt Colony history books, plus the stack of freshly printed pages. I stepped out onto the little front porch of the old rented cottage, and locked the door behind me.

In a few minutes, my cousin Janet Hargrove Judson pulled up in her maroon sedan in front of the gate to the picket fence surrounding my little cottage. My name, Caroline Hargrove Hamilton, was new and fresh on the mailbox. Janet tooted her car's horn and waved at me.

"You ready?" she called.

"Sure I am." I settled myself in the passenger seat and showed my stack of folders to Janet. "Wait until you see what I've found out about the Hargrove family since I moved here," I said.

"Other family branches, too, I reckon," Janet said cheerfully. "We've all been here for a long while. You'll see a lot of the same names when we get to the family cemetery."

"Well, I appreciate your help in getting me there. I want to draw a map of the dirt roads as we drive along so I can find my way around here a little better."

Janet and I, cousins forever, had not spent too much time

together until recently. After my husband Craig died in Houston, the friendships there dwindled away, and I retired from my public relations job. My sisters and my brother were still in Houston, but busy with their own jobs, families, lives. My mother lived in a condominium in Clear Lake, and she was busy too. I decided to move to the country, where aunts and uncles and cousins might have a little more time for me.

Janet had time for me. Her own children were growing up, one a senior in high school, one going to college out-of-town, one already working in Houston. They left her with lots of spare time. She seemed to enjoy helping me find my way here or there, and already knew a lot about the family history I was researching.

She parked her car in front of the Yorktown library. "You'll learn your way around here, Carrie," she said, calling me by my childhood name. "You should have come out here more when we were younger! You'd know your way around like we do. At least now, the county's got signs on the dirt roads. It's harder to get lost than it used to be."

I knew what she was referring to. Once I had been driving around on the county dirt roads, and had gone around in circles. That was before the days of cell phones, and I couldn't call for help. The car was almost out of gas before I finally found my way to a paved road with signs to the nearest small town.

We walked into the library and headed toward the counter. A light-skinned black woman sat behind it. Interesting; not many black people live here in the country. I know that from the census records and demographics I've been researching. Martha McNair, her name plate said. She was tall and thin, with her black hair swept into a neat bun. Her face was long and thin. She wore black slacks and a beige sweater, gold earrings, a little lipstick. "Can I help you?" she asked as Janet and I approached her check-out station.

"Could I see the book about family cemeteries in DeWitt County?" I asked. "It contains maps to their locations, a list of their graves, and some biographical information. I called here about it and was told it's on reserve. May I see it and copy a few pages?"

"Sure thing. I know right where it is. Somebody else looked at it yesterday." Martha McNair walked to a nearby shelf and brought the largest book to the counter. "Is this the one you want?"

I thanked her and took the book to a nearby copy machine; opened it to the Hargrove section. Someone had left a marker there. I copied a few pages and returned the book to the counter.

"You haven't been here too long, have you?" Janet was asking Martha. "I don't recall seeing you in high school, long ago as that was, or PTA either. Did you just move to town like my cousin Caroline?"

Martha grinned. "I guess so. I grew up in San Antonio and spent most of my life there. Recently I retired after twenty years at my library job, and I just decided to move to a smaller town and work at a smaller library."

Janet looked at her. "Um-hmm. And more?"

"I'm divorced, if that's what you mean. Quite some time ago. Two children, both in college. How about you?"

"Grew up here, three children, one in college and one in high school. One's already moved to Houston. I'm still married to Jordan Judson, Texas Aggie, that's why I drive a maroon car."

I couldn't help joining the conversation. "Texas A&M school color. I should have figured that out. Anyway, your story and mine are similar, Martha, except I came here from Houston. My dad was born and bred here, and he's buried in the Hargrove cemetery, along with his parents and some of his brothers. He died in Viet Nam. Mama raised me and my sisters and brother in Houston, but I remember visiting here such a long time ago. And I still have cousins like Janet, and aunts and uncles too."

"Do you like it here?'

"In a lot of ways. But it's different from a big city. Things to get used to."

"What kind of work did you do?"

"Journalism, in various ways. Worked on a newspaper, then

went into public relations. I only have one child, and she's finished college and found a job already," I said.

"Is your husband here with you?"

"No." I winced at the thought. "He died in a car accident two years ago." *That's why I couldn't stay in Houston in our old house. That's why I moved to Yorktown, to find another part of my family. Something significant to occupy my time.*

Janet must have read my mind. "Oh, you'll learn to love it here," she said gently. "You know you're welcome back to the family."

* * *

A few miles from Yorktown, Janet turned onto a red dirt road. A cloud of dust began to appear behind her car, and she slowed down. I took out my notebook and started to draw a map of the roads we were traveling.

"We're going through Oak Creek first, aren't we?" I asked.

"We'll go by Maury's house there," Janet said. "Then it's up the road a ways, over a wooden bridge, and a zig to the left."

Directions like that never helped me, but I worked on my map of the country roads as we drove. From Yorktown, we traveled down a paved highway, then turned onto a dirt road network that left DeWitt County, cut through Karnes County, and re-entered DeWitt County where the family cemetery was located.

The land looked so familiar. Flat, grassy, with a few large trees; cattle grazed on it behind barbed wire fences. Dense scrub brush covered other sections, at least near the fence lines. Wildflowers already bloomed, though not as many as usual. We'd had a drought the past year.

The dirt roads threaded around large ranches, with only a few houses scattered throughout the country. Though I couldn't yet find my own way around, with Janet driving, things felt familiar. Vivid memories of childhood visits to Grandma Gussie and my cousins churned forth. Janet was guiding me back into my father's family and its territory. She had been a childhood friend on my visits, and was becoming a good friend now.

Only two months ago, I had decided to leave Houston and move to DeWitt County. I couldn't handle living on a farm or ranch by myself—and anyhow, they're not easy to find for rent—so I leased a cottage in Yorktown, population about 2,000. All my relatives lived out of town, but not far from Yorktown. Janet was especially nearby.

I put my house in Houston up for rent and made the move, bringing some of my furniture and storing the rest. I made a special trip to Glen Haven Cemetery in Houston, visiting my husband's grave, and told him I'd remember him wherever I might go. A little bit of grief rolled from my shoulders; he seemed to say my departure was all right.

In Yorktown, my spirits rose. The cottage was comfortable, the friendship with Janet began to thrive, and I began to feel relaxed and happy. I decided to make a project of family history, and found it very intriguing to myself and Janet as well. We took to researching early Texas history along with family history, since the two are entwined. We are in the sixth generation of Hargroves in DeWitt County.

Janet and I are first cousins, and we look somewhat alike. We're both middle height and rather thin. I have dark brown hair and hazel eyes, but Janet's hair is blond and her eyes are blue. She wears makeup and I don't, but we dress somewhat the same. I've left my business suits in storage in Houston, and I wear slacks or jeans most of the time. Janet does too.

"What's on your mind?" Janet asked me, breaking my train of thought.

"Oh, just some of the family history," I said. "Things I've been working on lately."

"Well, we're getting close to the cemetery. How's your map coming along?"

"Oh, gosh. Not very well. I forgot to keep up with it. Maybe I can fix it on the way home."

Janet slowed her car to avoid a dust trail from a car just a little way ahead. She pulled up next to the chain-link fence beside the road and parked the car next to the gate.

"Some family cemeteries are way back in the woods, and some have been neglected," Janet said. "The historic societies are trying to recover them and fix them up. We've been using ours since 1850, and luckily this road was built right beside it. The cemetery was built on the family ranch—you know, a grant—a league and a labor —but the ranch was sold off eventually. Even so, we kept the family cemetery, and somebody has kept taking care of it. That used to be Maury's father, but Maury took it over recently when he retired. Gives him a project, something he likes to do. He keeps it up nicely, too."

I picked up my notebook and papers and looked at my cousin. "Well—this is it. I want to see my father's grave, and then look at all the others."

Approaching the gate, we noticed it was hanging open. "Your dad's grave is straight ahead," Janet said, pointing the way. She closed the chain-link gate behind us. "We don't keep this locked, but it's supposed to be closed."

We walked past a row of older graves and approached a line of plots with headstones for six brothers and their wives, some in use and some awaiting. One of them was my father's grave with an empty plot for his widow still beside it. "Mama will be here someday," I said. "She never got over him, you know, even though they were so young when he died."

"That's happened a lot in our family." Janet handed me a Kleenex to blow my nose. "So many wars the men died in, or were injured and still died early. The women kept on a-plugging away, raised the children, ran the farm, and lived on into their eighties. They're buried beside their husbands, but you can see the difference of their lifetimes in their dates of death."

"Well, let's take a look around. I haven't been here in ages."

"Let's start with our great-great-great-grandparents. Thomas Watson Hargrove, who settled in DeWitt Colony in 1825, and his wife, Mary Elizabeth Dennison. Their headstones are small but among the oldest. They're down this path, behind those bushes, and next to a patch of Cemetery Whites that might be in bloom by now."

"Cemetery Whites?" I hadn't heard of them.

"White irises. They're real old and hardy. They naturalize even in this climate."

We walked side by side, turning around the bushes and catching sight of the Cemetery Whites, a large patch in full bloom.

And then we caught sight of a large still man, lying down in the iris patch, a shovel beside him, grasped by his right hand. A large stain of dark red blood marked the front of his white shirt and spattered his woolen jacket.

We stopped in our footsteps and stared at the man.

He did not move.

"What's he doing here?" Janet whispered.

"He looks dead," I said.

"Probably dead. And it doesn't look like an accident. He looks murdered—don't you think?" Janet's voice shook as she spoke.

I walked slowly over to the body and reached out for the man's wrist. A few large blue flies buzzed away from his chest wound and his face. His eyes were wide open, staring, crusted and dry. His lips and fingernails had turned blue, cyanotic, losing oxygen as he bled. *But the skin of his face and arms is light brown, like Martha McNair's. He's a black man. What's he doing in our family cemetery?*

I didn't think that on purpose, but it came into my mind all the same. I touched his wrists. His skin was cold. There was no pulse.

It almost made me vomit. "Oh, my God! He *is* dead. Where's his murderer? Oh, let's get out of here. Let's get some help!"

"You're right." Janet reached for my hand, and we ran stumbling back onto the stone pathway leading to the fence, the

15

gate, Janet's maroon car. We scrambled into our seats and Janet started the engine, fingers shaking.

"We'll have to call the police and report this."

She turned the car around on the narrow road, then hit the accelerator, heading back to Yorktown. I took out my cell phone. Finally I managed to call 911 and someone answered.

"DeWitt County Constable's Office. Can I help you?"

"Yes," I said. "I want to report a dead man in the Hargrove Family Cemetery."

"A dead man *where*?"

"In the *cemetery*. It's not a funeral. A dead body. We think he was murdered. He must have been shot, or stabbed, some time ago."

"Ask for Constable Bennett!" Janet hissed.

"...so I need to report this to Constable Bennett, right now!"

* * *

It wasn't far down the road to our uncle's house. Janet pulled into the long driveway. "Hey!" she called to Uncle Cotton, who was in the large dog pen back of the barn. A hunting pack of twenty or so was kept there, and Cotton was in the enclosure feeding them.

When he saw us, Cotton quickly finished his feeding and exited the pen. He listened intently while we poured out our story, then led us to his pickup truck.

"Wait here," he said. "I'll get my rifle from the house."

He strode back and loaded the rifle into the truck's gun rack.

"Hop in," he said. "Let's go."

The truck sped down the red dirt road, and pulled up beside the cemetery fence. Two police cars were already parked there, and an ambulance was nearby. "There's Bob Bennett," Uncle Cotton said. The patch of Cemetery White irises, and the nearby graves, were marked off with yellow crime-scene tapes.

Cotton dismounted from the pickup truck. He strode into the family cemetery and walked up to Constable Bob Bennett. Janet and

I followed, distracted by two ambulance drivers who had zipped the dead man into a large black bag and were lifting him onto the folded-down stretcher. They strapped him into place, lifted up the bed, and rolled it toward the ambulance. With the dead man in the ambulance, they slammed the double doors shut and drove him away.

I stepped close to Uncle Cotton and Constable Bennett. "Who is that man? What was he doing here anyway?" I asked. Maybe they had already found out.

"How did he get here?" Janet chimed in. "There's no car parked around here. And why was he digging up our Cemetery Whites? They're old and unusual, but not *that* rare and valuable."

Constable Bennett looked uncomfortable, then said, "I guess I can tell you what we know so far. There was a wallet in the man's pocket, with a driver's license and other papers. Credit cards, money. His name was Thomas Harrison and his address is in San Antonio. Looks like he's a professor at San Antonio State University."

I couldn't help but moan. Learning someone's name and occupation gives him identity and existence, and gives you more reason to care about his loss.

Constable Bennett looked at me and said, "How he got here, and why, we still don't know, or why anybody would shoot him. All that's still on the burner. We have a lot to find out."

"Is there anything you need from us?"

"You can give your account of finding him. Talk to the officers when they finish examining the scene over there." Bennett called to his assistants and motioned them toward us.

"We'll find out something about what he was shot with soon," he said. "The body is going to the coroner's office, and the bullet will be extracted. It'll be sent to ballistics for examination."

"Maybe he *was* stealing iris bulbs," Janet said to the police officer writing things down. "Why else would he have dug some up with the shovel?"

A different thought came into my mind. I began to remember what Maury had said so long ago. Something about two bodies in one grave. He never said which one. Could it have something to do with Thomas Hargrove and his wife? Was that what Professor Harrison meant to dig up?

If this was still a family secret, would somebody shoot him over that?

Cemetery Whites

CHAPTER THREE

As Uncle Cotton drove Janet and me back to his house, I mulled over Maury's old story, but I didn't say anything about it. Maury had said that Grandma Gussie would skin him alive if he disclosed that information, and even though Grandma Gussie was dead and gone, I didn't want to get Maury into any trouble.

Even when Janet and I, with Janet's husband Jordan, joined cousin Maury and his wife Elizabeth at Yorktown's Stockman Restaurant, I said nothing about the double grave. Neither did Maury. The conversation focused on the murder victim—if he *had* been murdered, because it certainly looked as if someone had shot him; it didn't look like a suicide—and who he was, and how in the world he had ended up in the cemetery. There was no car or motorcycle to be found, so someone must have brought him there. Who could it be, and why?

I decided to speak to Maury privately as soon as possible. Maybe, all those years ago, he had just made up the story of two bodies buried together, and didn't even remember it today.

I focused on my chicken-fried steak, mashed potatoes, and green beans. After dinner, Janet drove me home. We agreed to meet again in the morning for breakfast and then a possible trip to the cemetery. We'd check first with Bob Bennett to make sure the yellow tapes had been removed and a trip was okay. Safe and okay.

But when Janet drove up to my house Wednesday morning, something had already changed.

"What's the matter?" I asked, climbing into the front seat. Janet looked upset, and there was a stack of newspapers in the back seat of her car.

"Oh, Lord!" Janet groaned. "Somebody let the cat out of the bag, and even the younger generation is against doing that, though not as much as the old folks were—still are, those that are still with us. You know what I'm talking about, don't you? The extra body in Thomas Hargrove's grave. Maury told me he told you about it years ago. It's a secret everybody knows, but doesn't discuss."

She parked the car in front of the breakfast restaurant, Casa Maria, and took two copies of the newspaper from the back seat. "We can read what they've written up while we're waiting to be served."

We settled down in a roomy, quiet booth with coffee to drink and breakfast on the way. We unfolded the newspapers. On the front page, there was a brief article about the death of Thomas Harrison, with a photo probably from his driver's license, and a referral to the Lifestyle section. The main feature story on the front page of the Lifestyle section contained three photos. Two of them were ancient portraits, one labeled "Thomas Watson Hargrove" and one "James Jamison". The third, biggest photo was taken yesterday in the Hargrove cemetery, when the yellow tape was still in place. A young man cradling a rifle stood inside the square of tape.

Above the article ran a headline. It read:

Is the Sutton-Taylor Feud Back Again?

"Oh, no," Janet sighed. "Just what nobody wants to hear."

"What does that mean?" I asked. "That feud ended over a hundred years ago, didn't it? What does it have to do with our cemetery?"

"That feud lasted for such a long time after the Civil War, and created so much terror. So many deaths, including some in our family." Janet took a sip of coffee. "Some people moved to other counties to avoid the vigilante groups. This happened during the

Reconstruction days, when there was a lot of animosity and little real law and order."

"Well, what's that got to do with the murder yesterday?"

"Oh, let's read the newspaper article. It will probably have something to say. That's Great-Aunt Hettie's grandson Donny there in the photograph, carrying a rifle. Or Danny. They're twins, remember. One of them must be the one who talked to the reporter."

The article read:

Two bodies may lie in the grave of Thomas Watson Hargrove, buried in the Hargrove Family Cemetery after he died on April 26, 1875. His funeral took place on April 27, almost one hundred and thirty-five years ago.

A rumor, never openly discussed, traveled through DeWitt County after the funeral. Just a few days before his death, Hargrove's grand-daughter Caroline Jane Hargrove Jamison had returned to her family's homestead. She left her husband, James Jamison, who was once again away from their ranch to ride with a Sutton vigilante group.

Jamison never returned to his ranch, and the reason behind his disappearance has never been verified. It was thought that, in pursuit of his estranged wife, Jamison may have traveled to the Hargrove homestead to retrieve her.

Perhaps he counted on the oncoming demise of Thomas Watson Hargrove, who was on his deathbed. His sons had already dug his grave in preparation for the funeral, and the Hargrove family might be distracted from Mrs. Jamison's needs because of Mr. Hargrove's forthcoming burial.

But perhaps the sons, including the father of Caroline Jane, heard the plans of Jamison. They may have laid in wait for him at the crossroads near their house.

The story goes that words were exchanged, and so were shots. Jamison fell to the ground. His horse ran away and his gold watch and gun fell into a patch of cactus. They were found months later.

Did Jamison die near the Hargrove homestead? Was he placed at the bottom of Thomas Watson Hargrove's grave, which was dug fresh and deep?

If so, the facts were never proven. The cemetery stood on family land, and guards prevented any access to the new grave both before and after the Hargrove funeral. The questions were suppressed and eventually abandoned during the following hundred-plus years.

Perhaps the truth was being sought by San Antonio State University history professor Thomas Harrison, who visited the cemetery yesterday. There he was fatally shot and left to die all alone.

He was found dead there yesterday morning, lying on the ground with a shovel in his hand, prepared to dig up the dual grave in search of historical proof.

Constable Bob Bennett of DeWitt County agrees that historical investigation may have prompted Harrison's visit to the cemetery. However, there are numerous other questions to be answered in solving his murder.

These include his transportation to the cemetery. His car was later found at a local motel, so someone must have driven him to the site of his death.

Any information would be appreciated by Constable Bob Bennett, by telephone or in person.

Constable Bennett's office phone number ended the story.

The Casa Rosa waitress arrived with breakfast. Two orders of *huevos a la Mexicana*, one served with jalapenos and one without. Janet opened the aluminum foil packet of tortillas, and we each took one, being careful because the tortillas were steaming hot.

I put beans and eggs on my tortilla then rolled it into a burrito. "Do you remember the red dust on the road ahead of us yesterday? I saw it when we parked. Someone was up ahead."

"Yeah, sure. But I didn't see anything *but* dust. Did you?"

"No—but Professor Harrison must have been dead for at least an hour before we arrived. Maybe his murderer stayed with him then drove off as we were coming down the road."

Janet's fork scraped up the last bit of refried beans from her plate. "Could be. Bob Bennett will figure it out. To tell the truth, I'm less concerned about the murder than I am about the reason for it. The two-body possibility has always been an embarrassment for the older generations. Uncle Cotton, Great-Aunt Hettie, Grandma Gussie when she was alive. Great-Aunt Laura, too. That's why it was supposed to be a secret." She took her second tortilla and rolled it up with butter and sugar inside. "By this time, it's been almost forgotten, especially by the family members who have moved away. Relocated to Houston or Dallas or San Antonio where they can find a job."

"Some come back," I protested.

Janet shrugged. "You're back, and I hope you stay. But not everyone returns. They change over the years, you know. And some things change here, too. Anyway, we'll have a family meeting tonight at Uncle Cotton's to discuss this newspaper article and the cemetery murder. Do you want to come? Jordan and I can stop and pick you up about six o'clock. Okay?"

"Sure. I'd appreciate the ride and the company. Do you still want to go to the cemetery this morning?"

"Yes, but let's stop by the library first. I want to see if there's a book on the Sutton-Taylor Feud."

We finished our breakfast and drove a few blocks to the library. Janet looked through the Texana section for something about the feud. I looked around for Martha McNair and found her shelving children's books.

Martha saw me and waved. "Just a minute," she said, and finished replacing a few more volumes, then walked to the check-out counter where Janet, with a book, and I were standing.

Connie Knight

"I'm glad you two stopped in," Martha said. "I read that article in the newspaper this morning, and there's something I wanted to tell you." She took Janet's book, checked it out, and handed it back. "That picture in the paper of Thomas Harrison? He's the one who was here on Monday, looking at the Texana section. He must have left that marker in the book you copied pages from—the one about the DeWitt County family cemeteries."

"Oh," I said. "Looking for information, just like me."

"He also asked to see county maps, but I didn't have any he wanted to copy. Then—and this is the interesting part—he asked if I knew anything about Henrietta Hargrove Harrell. She's related to you, isn't she?"

"Oh, yes. Great-Aunt Hettie. Did you tell him anything?" Janet put the library book into her large purse.

"I gave him a phone book, and he copied her address and phone number."

Janet and I looked at each other.

"I certainly hope that didn't cause any problems for your aunt."

"We'll see Aunt Hettie tonight," Janet said finally. "We can talk to her then. Maybe she met him and gave him some historical information."

Martha hesitated. "I called Constable Bennett and gave him this information, too. I thought he might find it helpful in some way."

"Mmm. Well, thank you," Janet said. I was quiet. "We appreciate your letting us know about it."

We walked from the library to the maroon sedan. Janet and I were both quiet.

"Maybe we'd better talk to Bob Bennett before we drive out to the cemetery," I finally said. "If one of Aunt Hettie's sons or grandsons had something to do with shooting Professor Harrison, I want to know about it. And I don't want to risk getting myself shot, either."

"Mmm. They wouldn't shoot a relative," Janet said. "But they might not recognize you. Maybe we should put the visit off. You'll meet Aunt Hettie and her family this evening."

"Are you sure I want to meet all of them?"

"Oh, yes. I don't really think they were involved with a murder, either. They might get into fist fights, and raise fighting roosters, and ride wild bulls in the local rodeos, but that's as feisty as they get. Really."

"Mmm."

"There's a historical cemetery in San Antonio. Want to go there tomorrow?"

"Well, that would be nice. Some of our family is buried there. Some had moved into San Antonio after the Civil War. I can research the records this afternoon, so we'll know who to look for."

"Jordan and I will pick you up at six o'clock this evening then, and we'll go to the family meeting."

* * *

Back at the cottage, I sat down at the trestle table in my study. It holds a dozen stacks of papers and books, organized by family lines or topics such as colonization, Civil War, demographics, census records, and historical museum events coming up.

I flipped idly through one set of papers and another. Searching Hargrove family history had taken me into other families whose young ones had married into the Hargroves, and into the history of the DeWitt and other Texas colonies.

In 1825, Americans started immigrating into the Texas colonies their empresarios created. Of course, Spain had established missions, towns, and roads in Texas for years before 1825, but the population was sparse. Now the government of Mexico, having achieved independence from Spain, wanted to produce growth in the area, to establish ranches and farms and prosperous towns too. Empresarios like Stephen Austin made contracts with Mexico allowing them to colonize large areas of land. Three hundred families settled in Stephen Austin's colony, with grants made along the Brazos River and other tributaries. His colonists planned to create rice, cotton, and sugar cane plantations, and brought slaves along for this purpose. Mexico didn't allow slaves, though. The slaves were known as bondsmen instead.

Farther inland, in the South Texas Plains, the DeWitt Colony was also established in 1825. There was only one slave in that colony, owned by James Kerr, an empresario partner of Green DeWitt. The colonists planned to use their land for ranches and family farms. DeWitt Colony was followed by other colonies. Those founded a few years later provided land to immigrants from Germany, Poland, Czechoslovakia, and Bohemia. They followed their European farming habits of work done by the family. The colonists purchased a league and labor of land—4,428 acres of grazing land for a ranch and 177 acres for a farm. They grew corn and other vegetables, raised hogs and cattle. Water was plentiful, so was wild game. The immigrants prospered over years to come. Families did their own work.

It didn't take long for the Texas colonists to decide to fight for independence from Mexico. In 1836, they—and many of the Mexicans who lived in Texas before the colonists arrived—fought in the Texas Revolution and helped establish the Republic of Texas. The Republic lasted until 1845, when Texas was annexed by the United States.

In 1861, the State of Texas seceded from the Union to join the Confederate States of America. Many farmers of the DeWitt Colony and the surrounding area opposed the secession of Texas, saw no point in fighting for slavery which they didn't believe in, or practice; but when it happened, they joined the Confederate Army and left home to fight.

Farm and ranch work was left in the hands of women, and so was defense against raids by Apache and Comanche Indians.

Shuffling through the papers on my trestle table, I found copies of letters written by my great-great-grandparents, John David Hargrove and his wife Sarah, during the Civil War.

Cemetery Whites

Sarah Gaines Hargrove and her daughter, Caroline Jane, had the help of the only two slaves in the family. Priscilla, seven years older than Sarah, had assisted her all her life, and had traveled to DeWitt County with her after Sarah married John David Hargrove during his youthful trip to Mississippi.

Priscilla's husband, Josiah Gaines, accompanied her to Texas, but he died along the way. Her only child, Willie, was two years older than Caroline Jane.

During the Civil War, Priscilla took care of Sarah and the household, while Willie and Caroline Jane, who were thirteen and eleven respectively when the war started, took care of the farm and the cattle. The farm was small and the cattle few, but it sustained the household.

When the war ended in 1865, Northern sympathizers called Radicals came into political power. Lawlessness and racial violence took over. The Sutton-Taylor Feud began in DeWitt County in 1866 with three Taylor men killing two black men and, in 1867, two Yankee soldiers. Deputy Sheriff William Sutton retaliated by killing Charley Taylor and James Sharp.

The Sutton side of the feud included many state police appointed to office by the Union military government. They proceeded to terrorize much of Southeast Texas. The Sutton-Taylor Feud lasted until 1880, despite a treaty signed in 1875. It continued to grow in the number of attacks on each side. Some people left the county to escape it; others stayed and were forced to choose sides. Staying neutral was impossible.

No wonder Caroline Jane left her husband to return to the Hargrove homestead, I thought. *He must have been crazy to side with the Suttons and ride vigilante with them. Maybe the war gave him post-traumatic stress syndrome. I wonder why Caroline Jane married him in the first place.*

I ruminated for a few more minutes. *Maybe that's why the double grave was such a family secret back then. The Sutton-Taylor Feud was reaching a treaty in 1875. Retaliation killings were supposed to end. If the Hargroves were held responsible for killing James Jamison—even if they had a good reason—the Sutton side might start things up again.*

The idea made me shiver.

They could have killed the whole family. Wiped us all out. Janet, Maury and I wouldn't be here today, because our ancestors would have been eradicated.

Ugh! I don't want to think about it anymore.

I slammed the notebook shut, walked into the living room, and turned the television on. I looked for something cheerful to watch. Maybe a sitcom, instead of anything about law and order.

CHAPTER FOUR

Promptly at six o'clock Wednesday, March 17, Janet and Jordan drove up to my little cottage, just as arranged. I was waiting on my front porch, wearing black wool slacks and a heavy red sweater. I carried a jacket. In March, the days in DeWitt County are much warmer than the nights, and I get cold easily.

I climbed into the back seat of the maroon sedan, and we set off for Uncle Cotton's house. Jordan did the driving, and kept the radio tuned at low volume to a San Antonio country music station.

"Who will attend the meeting tonight?" I asked Janet. Various relatives, scattered across several counties, might attend, including some I had never met before.

"Great-Aunt Hettie will be there, with David and Darryl, her sons who live with her. Also her grandsons, Donny and Danny, who live with her, too. Our other cousins who live around here will surely attend, and possibly David the lawyer and Allen the accountant will drive in from San Antonio. Wives and children will probably stay at home if the little kids are going to sleep early. Oh, Betsy Benson and her parents will be there. They're coming in from Cuero. I think Betsy is bringing her boyfriend from college. Carl's his name, I think. And maybe Lisa Hargrove. She wouldn't be playing with her band on Wednesday night. There might be others, too. I know more of them than you, but not everyone."

Soon we turned off the dirt road onto Uncle Cotton's long gravel driveway. There's a large parking area between his house and barn, and it was almost full. I could see a line of pickup trucks, old and new; sedans and SUVs; a Lexus, a Cadillac, and a Mercedes-Benz. There were three Harley-Davidson motorcycles, parked side by side. Jordan eased the maroon sedan into a spot close to the house. We left the car and hurried on in. A cold wind was blowing from the north, lowering the temperature rapidly.

Uncle Cotton lives in a large ranch-style house, built of brick. There's a back porch that can be opened in the summer or closed in the winter. We headed down a path to the double-door entry to the porch. Through the blinds and drapes we could see perhaps two dozen relatives in various groups, glad to see each other, talking about this and that to catch up on family news—not limited to the graveyard murder and the newspaper story.

Once in the house, we hung up our jackets and said hello to Uncle Cotton. He pointed us to a table of food and drink. "Help yourself. Maury and Elizabeth felt we needed some food at our meeting."

We filled our plates. I looked at people in the room and listened to their conversations.

An older woman with a wrinkled face was saying, "She's the hard-heartedest little thing I've seen in all my put-togethers. She won't budge a eench!"

A younger one was telling a joke I'd already heard about a Texas woman driving on I-10 in West Texas. She saw a young man sitting on the side of the road, holding a gun to his head. Appalled, she stopped her car and began to plead with him to spare his own life. No avail. Finally she realized she was in Crockett County, and she said to the young man, "Think of Davy Crockett. He wouldn't do what you're trying to do, now would he?"

The young man replied, "Who's Davy Crockett?"

The gracious Texas woman responded, "Well, bless your heart. Just go ahead and pull the trigger, you dumb ass son of a bitch."

The group listening to the joke burst into laughter. I drifted away and headed for Uncle Cotton, who was talking with my beautiful blond young cousin Betsy Benson and her college boyfriend Carl.

Carl spoke with a soft West Texas drawl. "Ah like to hunt with mah bow and arrah. Someday Ah want to hunt a javelina or two, but Ah believe they're out of season by now."

Uncle Cotton looked uncomfortable, and Betsy made it worse. "Uncle Cotton hunts those wild hogs year round, now don't you?" she said. "Why is that, Uncle Cotton?"

"The ranchers hire me to shoot those hogs when they're rooting up the ranch pastures and making potholes in the ranch roads. Been doing it for years whenever they ask me to."

Carl asked, "Isn't it dangerous to hunt them down where they live? Their tusks are razor-sharp, aren't they?"

"Sometimes they get one of my dogs, but they haven't got me."

"What do you do with them when you kill them, Uncle Cotton?" Betsy asked. "Are they okay to eat, or do they carry leprosy like armadillos can?"

"I don't eat them. They stink. I feed them to my dogs."

Uncle Cotton seemed uncomfortable and backed himself into a corner. Cousin David the lawyer rescued him unwittingly by tapping a spoon on a glass to gain everyone's attention.

"It's almost seven o'clock, and tonight's a week night. Lots of us have to wake up early in the morning and go to work. Let's get on with our meeting now, shall we? Okay if I preside again?"

David had run meetings before. Nobody objected. He said, "There are two reasons for the meeting tonight. The first one is concern about the man who died in our cemetery. The second one is the newspaper article about our cemetery. Let's start with the first one. Does anybody know anything about Professor Thomas Harrison? Why he might be digging at the foot of Thomas Hargrove's grave? Why anyone would shoot him?"

Silence. Great-Aunt Hettie had probably been contacted by the professor, but she didn't say a thing. I looked at Janet across the room and raised my eyebrows. She shook her head slightly, so I didn't say a thing either.

31

Lawyer David waited another minute. "Well," he said. "We know one of us participated in the newspaper article. Was that you, Donny? How did that happen?"

Donny was indignant. "That wasn't me; it was Danny."

Danny and Donny were identical twins, and both lived with their grandmother Hettie. Donny clutched Hettie's hand and said, "You better ask my brother. I got nothing to say."

Danny, sitting on the other side of Hettie, leaned forward and said defensively, "Yeah, I talked to the reporter. He came by the house and I was the only one there. Grandma and Donny had gone somewhere that morning and they hadn't come back yet."

He took a sip from his bottle of beer. "The reporter didn't know anything about Professor Harrison. He'd heard about the double grave and wanted to write an article about it. So I told him what I know, and I took Grandma's old rifle to use in the picture he wanted to take. We drove to the cemetery, and it surprised us both to see the yellow tape in the graveyard. It was after three o'clock in the afternoon, and nobody else was there. We took our pictures and left."

The feature article appeared the next day in the Lifestyle section of the newspaper as had probably already been planned. A brief—surprising—article on Professor Harrison's death appeared on the newspaper's front page. To me, Danny seemed to be telling the truth.

More silence. David said, "So then, what do we want to accomplish? The old family rumor has been published. That's a cat out of the bag, and we can't abolish it. But maybe keeping it secret isn't as important as it used to be. Maybe we don't have to worry too much about the newspaper article. The Sutton-Taylor Feud ended so long ago I don't think it's going to start up again.

"Next, there's the death of Professor Harrison. What's that got to do with us, except it happened on our territory? We didn't do anything, did we? Or initiate a murder committed by someone else?"

The group remained silent. "Of course not. We didn't want these things to happen. We weren't alive back in 1875 when the unknown man may—that's *may*—have been buried with Thomas Hargrove, and we don't know much about Professor Harrison."

He looked around the room. "For myself, I'd like to find answers to any questions, to resolve any issues, to clear any infamy from our family name. Do you agree?"

The silent crowd burst into a voice of agreement.

"But we don't want Thomas Hargrove dug up," someone objected. "We'd like to know if somebody's in the grave with him, and if so who it is, but we don't want to disturb him. Anyway, even if there is a second skeleton in the grave, what could we learn to tell us who that might be? That stuff you see on TV shows probably wouldn't work on a corpse from 1875, would it?"

The crowd agreed again.

David tapped the spoon on his glass for order. "You're right," he said. "I agree. I've been thinking we might take another route. For one thing, the current murder is more important. I'd like it solved. We don't want to think that a second person copying Professor Harrison would try digging up our graveyard, do we?"

In response came another rumble of agreement.

"So maybe we should hire a detective to assist Constable Bennett's office in investigating the death of Professor Harrison?"

This time, there was silence. *How much will this cost?* people were thinking. *How productive will the detective be?*

After a minute, I said, "David, Janet and I are driving to San Antonio tomorrow. Maybe we could investigate Professor Harrison. Check his house, talk to his neighbors. Want us to try that before we hire anyone?"

A moment of silence, a murmur of approval. Janet looked at me and nodded her head in agreement.

"Any objection?" David asked.

There wasn't.

"I'm researching family history, too," I added. "If I find

anything out about the double grave, I'll let everyone know. But not the newspaper."

Another buzz of approval brought an end to the meeting. Some cousins gathered in clusters to talk, and others put on their jackets and said good-bye.

Janet and Jordan sought me out; they were ready to go home.

So was I.

"Do you still want to drive to San Antonio after breakfast tomorrow morning?" I asked Janet.

"Oh, why not," she responded. "There's the historic cemetery to visit, and plenty of other things to do. Where will we go to check on Professor Harrison?"

"I'll find out," I said. "I'll make a list. Places to go, people to see, things to do, et cetera. We can be a couple of Little Rascals."

Janet remembered the rhyme from Our Gang movies on TV and laughed. "Pick you up at nine and have breakfast before we leave town?" she asked.

"Sounds fine. I'll be ready."

Jordan turned a corner and soon pulled his car up before my cottage. The porch light burned brightly and made the house look friendly to me.

Jordan and Janet waited as I walked to my front door, opened it, switched on the living room light. I waved good-bye, and they drove away.

I set down my purse and newspaper, wandered into the kitchen, and made myself a plate of cookies. The day's tension drained away. In my study, I took a legal tablet of yellow, lined paper and wrote a header: "Things to Do".

First, in San Antonio, we could do more family research. Confederate veteran John David Hargrove and wife Sarah had moved from the ranch into the city around 1880, and were buried in the old city cemetery, not in the country. Their two-story Victorian house still stood, I'd heard, and had been restored by the current owners.

Cemetery Whites

Then, to find information about Thomas Harrison, we could stop by his house—or apartment—and talk to his neighbors, then stop by the university and locate his office. See if anyone was there to talk to. It's still spring break.

I could check the Internet at home, too. See if there was anything on it about Thomas Harrison.

Also—and I'd certainly need Janet's help with this—we ought to talk to Great-Aunt Hettie. Professor Harrison had her name and address. Did he contact her? Did she tell him about the double grave? Does she know anything about him, about his reasons for digging in our cemetery?

She had kept quiet at the family meeting, but to me she looked like she could have had something to say.

I'd been a journalist and a public relations practitioner in the past, after all.

I still know how to make people talk.

For now, I'd make the computer talk. It was not quite eight-thirty in the evening, and I had plenty of energy left. I entered the study and looked at the desk with the computer vs. the trestle table with stacks of books and documents.

The computer won. I logged in and began a search for information about Professor Thomas Harrison in San Antonio.

The basic facts weren't hard to find. He owned a house on Burleson Street in Dignowity Hill, an area included in the National Historic Registry of Neighborhoods. Old houses there have been bought and restored, like those in many other historic neighborhoods in San Antonio. Dignowity Hill is on the East Side of San Antonio, near downtown, and near the forty-acre historic city cemetery where my great-great-grandparents, John David and Sarah Gaines Hargrove, are buried. Maybe the two-story house they built is in Dignowity Hill too. Or somewhere nearby. I've heard it was built on Rattlesnake Hill, but that could be the same place as Dignowity Hill, just with a different, older name.

With an address for Professor Harrison in hand, I logged off the computer and moved to the trestle table. A notebook of family-tree material, copied from documents prepared by cousin Miranda, awaited me. Letters, deeds, newspaper articles, and records of family branches descended from Thomas Watson Hargrove crammed the various sections, rich with information new to me.

Thomas Watson Hargrove and his wife Mary Elizabeth Dennison came to DeWitt Colony from Missouri in 1825, and settled with a league and a labor of land for a ranch and a family farm. John David Hargrove was their first child, born in Texas, and followed by several more. John David was my direct ancestor, and Janet's, too. He and Sarah Gaines created several children: Caroline Jane, Thomas, David, George, and then Sarah Amanda, who died at the age of three.

I riffled through Miranda's papers and found an account she had written about Caroline Jane.

During the Civil War, John David Hargrove, his brothers and even his father, joined the Confederate Army in 1861 and went off to fight. Left behind were Sarah (sickly at that time) her young sons, and her daughter Caroline Jane, and Sarah's household slave Priscilla and her son Willie. Priscilla and Willie had come to Texas with Sarah when she married John David. Seven years older than Sarah, Priscilla had taken care of her—been her nanny—since Sarah was born. She took care of the frail Sarah during the Civil War, and the diminished household, while Caroline Jane and Willie managed the garden, the milk cow, the pigs, the chickens, and more; they hunted wild game and provided plenty of food for the family. Caroline and Willie also both used rifles to defend the household against Indian raids.

John David and Sarah exchanged long, frequent letters. His wife saved John David's letters, and he saved those of hers that he could. Sarah took pride in the work of Caroline Jane, and Willie, too. He was the older child, tall and strong, courteous and industrious. Just as Sarah had taught Priscilla to read and write when they were growing up together, Priscilla taught the skills to her son Willie and also Caroline Jane. They shared reading the Bible, other books in the house, newspapers and letters, too.

In 1865, when the Civil War soldiers straggled home, Caroline Jane was fifteen years old. Two years later, at the age of seventeen, she married James Jamison. He was several years older than she.

Her brothers were establishing their farms and ranches near the homestead of their parents, but James Jamison moved to a desolate area some miles away, far from any neighbors. Willie, now a free man, still lived on John David's farm. He moved with James and Caroline Jane to help set up the new Jamison ranch. His mother, Priscilla, remained with John David and Sarah.

The ranch and farm became successful, but its distance from neighbors perhaps accounts for James Jamison's activities with the Sutton-Taylor Feud (1866-1880). In her husband's frequent absence, Caroline Jane took over management of the farm and the ranch, hiring and housing some former slaves to work there. Willie became her foreman/manager.

The ranch and farm prospered, but the marriage failed. Caroline Jane became more independent, and it drove her husband into domineering behavior and physical abuse. Eventually, Caroline Jane decided to leave her husband and return home. Her husband pursued her, but he disappeared and never returned. Caroline Jane eventually moved to New Mexico with her brother Tom.

Moved away from Texas. I hadn't read about that before.

I set Miranda's article down and looked at the clock on the wall above my desk. Almost ten. Time to watch the news, time for a shower, time for a bedtime snack. Time for a good night's sleep. Tomorrow would be another busy day. Time to get ready for it.

CHAPTER FIVE
Thursday, March 18, 2010

Janet picked me up at nine o'clock and we headed for Casa Rosa for breakfast. Constable Bob Bennett was already there, sitting in a large booth. He brightened at the sight of us, and we headed toward his table. "Join me?" he asked, and we did. He smiled at me and moved his newspaper and notebook from the table.

Janet and I sat opposite him. The waitress came and poured our coffee, took our orders. I couldn't help paying some attention to Bob Bennett, who shifted until he was sitting right across from me, even though he was talking to Janet. He wore a starched uniform with a constable's badge. Somehow it emphasized his broad shoulders, his muscular build. His dark brown hair was parted on the left side and combed to the right, but a shock of it fell over his forehead. His eyes were clear and brown. His hands around the coffee cup were large and strong. No wedding ring could be seen.

Absence of a wedding ring snapped me out of my dreamy state of mind. I didn't wear a ring either. Bob Bennett was attractive, but he didn't look at all like Craig Hamilton, my darling husband who was gone. I didn't want to cry remembering him. Resolutely, I set aside thinking about Craig's loss and began to listen to Bob and Janet. Professor Harrison's family in San Antonio had been contacted, Bob said, but the body had not yet been released. The family was still making funeral arrangements.

I tried to think of a question to ask so I could take part in the conversation. "Has the autopsy been completed? Has the bullet been removed and identified?"

Bob turned from Janet to me. "Yes, it has. The bullet was fatal; no poison, no heart attack, no mysterious cause of death. There's a problem, though. We don't know whose gun it came from, or who shot it."

"No suspects?" I tried not to sound too hopeful, but the prospect of Great-Aunt Hettie's elimination as a possible culprit cheered me.

"No real suspects." Bob's voice was cautious. "We're asking around, but so far haven't found out much. The professor has been here a few times lately, staying at the same motel, but what that has to do with the shooting isn't apparent."

Bob's cell phone rang. He answered it, spoke briefly, then hung up and sighed. "Back to work," he said. He stood up and donned his black leather jacket. "Have a nice day in San Antonio, ladies. Please let me know if you find out anything about Professor Harrison."

He gave me a smile, paid his bill at the cash register and was gone.

Janet and I finished our *huevos a la Mexicana* and soon were on the road to San Antonio. I basked in the sunlight that warmed the passenger seat. Janet focused on driving for a while, then looked at me and said, "Bob and Jordan are lifelong friends, you know. They went to school together, played football together in high school, went to Texas A&M together. They both studied agriculture, both took over their family farm, both have other jobs to supplement the income from farming. The only difference is that Jordan and I are still married, but Bob's wife left him a dozen years ago. She moved to Houston and took the children with her. Bob's been living alone ever since."

She shot me a questioning glance. "You two seemed a little interested in each other. That's why I'm telling you this."

I felt my cheeks flush, and I replied carefully, "I do think he's attractive, and, yes, he seemed a little interested in me."

"Well, he must be," Janet said. "He doesn't usually pay attention to any woman, but he has to you."

I said nothing. My tongue was tied.

Janet continued, "He goes to church where we do. You ought to join us, Caroline. The church community is important here. Lots of activities, lots of ways to meet people and make friends."

"Well, I already do know Bob," I said.

"Yes, but you'd see more of him if you came to church. Other people, too, for friends. That librarian is interesting, isn't she? Martha McNair, I mean. She attends our church and sings in the choir. I'd like to know her better, wouldn't you? Maybe we could invite her to lunch or dinner sometime."

"Isn't Lisa Hargrove's band playing Friday night?" I asked. I'd heard about a barbecue restaurant in Cuero, the county seat. It featured country and bluegrass bands on the weekends. Pool tables and a little dance floor complemented good food and music.

"She plays in Cuero every Friday nowadays. Well, we could invite Martha. See if she's interested."

"*I'm* interested," I said. "Would you and Jordan go there with me and Martha McNair if she wants to go too?"

"Oh, why not," Janet said. "Jordan likes the place, and we haven't heard Lisa's band in a while. I'll ask Jordan when we get home tonight."

We were approaching San Antonio's Loop 410. We set the conversation aside as we entered the Loop. I consulted the map and navigated us to the appropriate exit, then to New Braunfels Street. We headed toward the huge, historic city cemetery, forty acres divided into twenty-nine separate sections. There we'd find the graves of our great-great-grandparents. Possibly other Hargroves, too, who hadn't been discovered yet in Miranda's papers.

We turned left from New Braunfels Street, looking for a place to park. The cemetery was several blocks deep and many blocks wide. It's shaped irregularly, bordered by New Braunfels, Pine Street, Crockett Street, and Palmetto, among others. The King of Spain gave the forty-acre land grant to the City of San Antonio, and it was subdivided into cemetery sections many years later.

Confederate veterans bought section number four in 1885 and it became known as the Confederate Cemetery. Nearly a thousand Confederate veterans and their dependents are buried there, along with later descendants and veterans of World War I and World War II.

A parking place wasn't hard to find. We left the car on a side street and started walking down the sidewalks. A cemetery map from cousin Miranda's packet led us to the Hargrove grave site, not too far from the curbside. A headstone of lustrous pink granite bore the names of John David Hargrove and Sarah Elizabeth Gaines Hargrove, along with the dates of their births, deaths, and marriage. Janet and I stopped beside the headstone, read the inscription and dates out loud. I felt humbled doing so. Here were settlers of early Texas, my ancestors, whose history should be more than merely a past-time to me. They deserved respect and honor. They, and their friends and relatives, helped to form the world we live in today. I said a silent prayer for them, and decided I ought to start going to church with Janet. She attended a historical church in Yorktown, built in the early DeWitt Colony days.

"We should have brought some flowers," Janet said.

"Next time, we will," I agreed. Just then, a man wearing a uniform and a name tag walked by, and an idea popped into my head. I ran after him. "Excuse me," I called. "Are there any records of burials here? Maybe there are more of my relatives here than I have on my list."

We followed him to a little stone hut. It contained volumes with hand-written pages, cabinets with index cards, and a computer. The employee, Felipe, sat down at the computer and looked up the names we gave him. No additional Hargroves, but there was a Gaines. Priscilla Gaines was buried in a section of the cemetery established for black people in the 1850s.

Janet and I followed Felipe's directions and walked some distance to see Priscilla's grave. I told Janet her history of coming to Texas as Sarah's slave, taking care of her for so many years, and then moving to New Mexico with Caroline Jane after James Jamison disappeared.

We finally found Priscilla's small gray slab with her name and dates. "I didn't know she came back to Texas," I said. "It wasn't in Miranda's papers—not those I've read so far."

"I never knew about her at all," Janet admitted. "But she was important in the family, too, wasn't she? From what you just told me, Sarah might not have survived the Civil War if Priscilla hadn't been there to take care of her."

I thought about Priscilla's history. "She had a son who came to Texas with her. I don't know what happened to him after the Jamison ranch fell apart. He had been the foreman there, according to the account of Miranda. His name was Willie. Maybe he moved to San Antonio?" Looking at Priscilla's grave, I felt like tracing her descendants. Maybe I could at least find out what happened to Willie.

"He might have moved to the East Side of San Antonio," Janet said. "Maybe Ellis Alley. That was a haven for former slaves. I hear it's been fixed up by a historical society, and I'd like to see it, but I don't think we have time today. I wouldn't mind coming back another day, though. There's a lot to see in San Antonio."

We said a silent farewell to Priscilla and returned to Janet's car parked near New Braunfels Street.

"Where next?" she asked.

I looked at the map. We were closest to Professor Harrison's house on Burleson Street. "Let's go there," I said. "Afterwards, we can drive by the Hargrove house on Sherman Street. It's not too far away."

Janet put her pedal to the metal, and off we went.

We ended up on Hackberry Street, heading north, and passing street signs for Brown Alley, Booker Alley, and Armadillo Alley. We passed by Dignowity Park, with huge elaborate houses on each corner across the streets that surrounded the park.

The Dignowity neighborhood stretched over many blocks.

Some houses were renovated, others were dilapidated. Some were large two-story mansions, others were small cottages. The area reminded me of the Houston Heights thirty years ago, when renovation there first started. By now, most sections of the Heights have been redone or rebuilt. Progress in San Antonio was coming along more slowly.

We easily found the Harrison house on Burleson Street. It sat on the corner of a block of old houses that have been restored. Large old trees graced the yards, and rose bushes were already in bloom. At Professor Harrison's Victorian house, a brick driveway led to a two-story garage with an upstairs apartment in the back yard. Janet parked her car on the street because a sleek black Mercedes-Benz already occupied the driveway.

The two of us looked at each other. "Let's give it a try," I said, and gathered up my purse, notebook and pen, and a small tape recorder—interview tools from my journalism job. We left the car and slowly, guardedly, approached the garage apartment. We had begun to hear a heated conversation.

A tall, thin young man ran his hand through his straight blond hair. "Whatever you folks decide to do about selling the house, I still have a lease on the garage apartment. Doesn't that mean anything to you? I can't take the time to move anywhere right now. I'm writing my dissertation, for God's sake, and that's already in trouble with Professor Harrison gone. He was my mentor, for God's sake!"

A young black woman in an elegant business suit replied to him in a quiet, calm voice. We couldn't hear what she said. She handed the young man a business card and turned toward us, walking to her car.

She saw us and frowned. "Are you here about my brother?" she asked abruptly. We looked at her, but before we could make an answer, she continued, "If he owes you some money, don't worry about collecting it. We're taking care of his funeral first, then selling his house and paying off his bills. Just send an invoice to this house, addressed to me, and I will take care of it." She handed us each a card, then got into her Mercedes-Benz and motioned for us to get out of her way. She backed out of the driveway and drove off.

We stood beside the driveway, staring at the cards. Estelle Shawn, Attorney at Law, they read. The young blond man walked down the driveway toward us.

"I'm Gregory Jackson, teaching assistant to Professor Harrison," he said. "At least I was until he died. Now I don't know what will happen. Can I help you with anything?"

His voice, his eyes, showed a streak of despair. "Professor Harrison was helping you in school?" I asked, making my voice quiet and slow. "You are working on your doctorate?"

He nodded. "Almost finished, if he was still here. I did all the research under his direction and wrote up my dissertation—most of it. Just need to finish it up this semester and have the committee approve it, and do my oral exam. Harrison would have led those procedures. Besides that, I had a job as his teaching assistant, and I still live in his garage apartment. If only he hadn't started gambling! His life is gone, and mine is collapsing, because of a flock of fighting chickens in the country. For God's sake, if he'd only stuck to common sense in his way of doing things."

He blinked back tears from his eyes.

"Gambling?" I asked.

"He just started a couple of years ago," Gregory said. "I haven't told anyone about it, but now that he's gone—maybe I shouldn't tell you, but it's churning in my mind—you seem interested, and you don't look like a gambler's hit man—anyway, before gambling, he always focused on his work, my research, his family. He never married anyone, but his relatives really mattered to him. My dissertation and his family were related, you might say. My research covered the changes in the lives of former slaves in this part of Texas during the late 1800s following the Civil War. That included Professor Harrison's family, who moved to San Antonio and did very well. What I found out, and shared with him, seemed to change his way of thinking. He started acting like Chicken George in Alex

Haley's *Roots*. Not that he raised his own roosters. He started spending time in DeWitt County and nearby areas, where roosters are raised and cockfighting takes place."

He shivered. "I haven't told this to his family, or anyone else."

"You can tell us." I patted his arm to soothe him. The three of us walked toward a wrought-iron table with matching chairs placed in the shady back yard. We each took a seat, and I introduced myself and Janet. "We're from DeWitt County, and Professor Harrison died in our family cemetery. He was digging something up, and somebody shot him. Do you have any idea who might have shot him? Some people think he was looking for a second body in my great-great-great-grandfather's grave. Does that seem likely to you?"

He wrung his hands and placed them over his face. "I think it must have had to do with gambling. He started going to cockfights out of curiosity, but then he started placing bets. Lately he's had a streak of losing money, and he's been harassed about paying debts. His sister Estelle has gone through his mail and found bills for credit cards, bank loans, and other loans too. Must have had to do with his gambling, but I didn't tell her anything about that. Not yet anyway. What he was trying to accomplish by digging in the cemetery, I have no idea, but maybe one of the gambling people shot him."

"Could be," I agreed. "They usually try to get money, though, don't they? Rather than taking your life?"

"I'm not an expert." Gregory's voice was dull. "Look, thank you for listening to me, but I'd appreciate it if you keep what I said to yourselves. The family is coming to grips with his death, and I'm working with the university about my job and my doctorate. I don't want to jeopardize anything."

"Oh, we won't tell anyone." I crossed my fingers behind my back. Telling Bob Bennett couldn't be avoided. "Anything else you want us to know?"

He shook his head, but brought a pad of paper and a pencil

Connie Knight

from the garage. All three of us exchanged names, addresses, and phone numbers.

"Good luck with finishing your doctorate," I told Gregory. He smiled wanly in response. Janet and I shook his hand good-bye and walked back to the maroon car.

I settled in the passenger seat, stowed my purse, and buckled the seat belt. "We've got a report for Bob Bennett. He must already know about the cockfighting cartel—if there is one."

"We have to visit Aunt Hettie before we see Bob," Janet said. "We want to ask her about any contact with Professor Harrison. Besides, her sons Darryl and David, plus the grandsons Donny and Danny, have all been involved in cockfighting from time to time. I don't know what they're up to now, but we need to find out."

"You mean find out anything they know about Professor Harrison's gambling?'

"Yep."

"Makes sense. They might know something useful. Are we still driving to Sherman Street to find John David and Sarah's house?"

"Yep." She put the key in the car's ignition and started it up. "Let's find the house, but this time, let's just drive by. It's time to head home now to beat the rush-hour traffic around here. Besides, Christopher will be home for dinner tonight. I've hardly seen him on this spring break; he's spent so much time with his high school friends."

In a few minutes, we stopped in front of a two-story stone house on Sherman Street. In my notebook, there was a folder holding a handful of photographs—copies of the old ones in Miranda's possession—that showed the old house and its street number, so we knew we were in the right place.

"It looks a lot like the original." I held out the photos so Janet could see them. "The iron fence is different now, and the trees are huge, but the structure is the same."

"It looks new. That means it's been restored, refinished. Otherwise, it would probably be falling apart. Wasn't it built about

Cemetery Whites

1880?"

"Just about." The solid old house impressed me. "Maybe we can meet the current owners sometime soon. I'd like to see the interior, if it's okay with them. Some people restore the original interior; others tear down the walls and make it contemporary inside. I hope it's original inside."

"Anyway, we'd better head home." Janet drove us back onto New Braunfels Street, and we retraced our way home on the same roads that brought us.

It wasn't quite three o'clock when we reached DeWitt County. Janet drove us to Aunt Hettie's house, located near Yorktown. It was on a dirt road, but just half a mile from the nearest paved county road. Aunt Hettie's house looked a lot like the one that had belonged to Grandma Gussie—a big square building, painted white, with a long front porch and a tin roof. There were chicken coops off to one side, a vegetable garden getting started on the other. There was probably a smokehouse in back of the house, maybe a barn with dairy cattle. Maybe a pig pen, too.

We didn't have to knock on the front door. Aunt Hettie had seen us. She opened the door and invited us in—rather reluctantly, it seemed. We followed her into the large front room. The television was tuned to a *Law and Order* re-run, and one of the identical twins was watching it, seated on a sofa across the room. He stood up, welcomed us, and identified himself as if it were often necessary. "Come on in, Janet and Caroline. I'm Donny."

Aunt Hettie led us to a table in the large kitchen. "I just made a pot of coffee. Would you like some?" Donny turned the TV off and joined us at the table. We settled in with our coffee, cream, and sugar, talking about our trip to San Antonio. Aunt Hettie added a plate of cookies. Finally she sat down in the last empty chair and fixed herself a cup of coffee. She looked at us, but said nothing. She was waiting for us to ask questions, if we had any. Silence fell upon the table.

Janet gave me a pointed look. I took a deep breath and

reminded myself to act like a journalist.

"Aunt Hettie, Janet and I are trying to find information about Professor Harrison. When you were across the kitchen getting our cups of coffee, you probably heard us telling Donny about our trip to San Antonio earlier today. We went to the professor's house and talked to the teaching assistant who lives in the garage apartment there. He told us quite a bit. And yesterday morning, when we stopped by the library, someone there told us Professor Harrison had asked about you. He looked you up in the telephone book. Aunt Hettie, did he get in touch with you?"

Aunt Hettie's face was grim. "The person at the library must have told Constable Bennett, too. He was here a couple of hours ago, asking me the same question."

"What did you tell him?"

"Nothing. I ain't got nothing to say."

Donny intervened. "She ain't got nothing *bad* to say. The professor called us and asked for help getting to the cemetery. Something about his history project. That's all."

"And what did you tell him, Aunt Hettie?"

Donny answered my question. "We said we'd take him. The reason is, I had met him at a rooster fight before. Once or twice. He was a nice guy. We didn't expect any problems."

"But I packed my pistol, just in case," Aunt Hettie said. "Donny knew him, but I didn't."

"Then she shot him by accident. Professor Harrison attacked her with his shovel to knock her gun out of her hands, and I bumped into her trying to get the shovel. The gun went off when she fell to the ground."

Aunt Hettie and Donny both seemed relieved at talking about the episode. "I wouldn't have pulled my gun on him if he hadn't been digging up the grave," Aunt Hettie said.

"The gun went off twice," Donny remembered. "Did they find two bullets in Harrison's chest? If they find two bullets, it makes it look like you did it on purpose. That's why I think we should keep

Cemetery Whites

our mouths shut, and not say anything to Constable Bennett."

"It didn't go off twice!" Aunt Hettie said indignantly. "I counted the bullets when we got home, and only one was missing."

"Why did you do that, Aunt Hettie?"

"I thought I heard two shots, too, but there must have been only one. Maybe we heard an echo. Only one of my bullets was missing."

All four of us looked at each other.

"Or there could have been another gun. How in the hell did that happen?"

"Who would have carried the second gun? Maybe a gambling hit man?"

"Wouldn't the two bullets be different? Did they both hit Professor Harrison? Would Bob Bennett have this information?"

We looked at each other again.

I said carefully, "Aunt Hettie, I can talk to Bob Bennett this evening and see what he has to say. Would you and Donny be willing to talk to him in the morning? Maybe we can clear you from having shot Professor Harrison. It might not be your bullet. Even if it is, there must be some way around being charged with anything. You didn't shoot the gun on purpose."

"I'm a witness to that," said Donny. "Just come talk to us in the morning and let us know what Bob Bennett has to say. Then we'll decide if we want to go talk to him."

I agreed.

"We're trusting you." Donny and Aunt Hettie looked at me. "Don't tell him anything. Just see what you can find out."

I shook Donny's hand and agreed.

Janet and I said our goodbyes and walked to the maroon sedan.

"Where do you think Bob Bennett will be this evening?" I asked.

"Try the steakhouse at dinner time. Otherwise, just try his cell phone. It's in the phone book."

"Steakhouse sounds better."

Connie Knight

Janet dropped me off at my cottage. We'd meet for lunch tomorrow, after I met with Aunt Hettie and Donny. Janet had a dental appointment in the morning, and then she'd go by the library and invite Martha McNair to join us Friday night.

"You'll be all right?" Janet asked.

"Yes. Thanks." My car needed some exercise, and I needed to drive around on my own just a little. "Let's meet at Aunt Hettie's about eleven, when your appointments are done. Then, if Aunt Hettie and Donny agree, we can accompany them to Bob Bennett's office."

"Sounds fine. You'll have to do the talking, though. After a trip to the dentist, my mouth stays numb for an hour. I won't be able to say anything. Guess I'll have to write an invitation for Martha McNair."

I laughed. "Well, that'll be different." I gathered my purse and notebook and headed for the cottage door. I wanted to change into nicer clothes before looking for Constable Bennett at Stockman Restaurant.

CHAPTER SIX

Seven o'clock seemed like a good time for dinner at Stockman's Restaurant. I upgraded my attire, changing into navy blue gabardine slacks, an ivory turtleneck shirt, and a beige suede jacket. The March night was becoming chilly. I found a tube of lipstick on my dresser and decided to put some on, and a little more makeup too. Then, gathering purse and notebook, I headed for my car and drove a few blocks to the steakhouse.

The large restaurant was crowded and noisy, but from the entry I saw Bob Bennett sitting at a table in the back of the room. As I walked toward him, he raised his head and saw me. His face brightened up, and he waved at me. I walked to his table and joined him.

"It's nice to share a meal with you again. I have lots of news for you from the San Antonio trip. Will you be able to stay here for a while for discussion?"

"I just ordered dinner, and I'm off duty, so sure, I can stay. What did you find out?"

The waitress brought us coffee and a basket of French bread with pats of butter. I told Bob about the trip to Professor Harrison's house in San Antonio's historic East Side district, and about his teaching assistant Gregory Jackson and his sister Estelle Shawn. "She's an attorney and she gave me her card."

"I've been talking to her by phone. She's making the family arrangements for Harrison's funeral in San Antonio. They have a family cemetery, too. Or, rather, a family plot in their church cemetery."

"Mmm. Maybe Janet and I can attend, if Ms. Shawn will allow it."

Bob looked intrigued, and I explained, "She thought we might be debt collectors, and I didn't have a chance to talk about the Hargrove cemetery. I'm sorry her brother died there, but I don't think it was our family's fault." Especially not Aunt Hettie and Donny. I kept this thought to myself.

I recounted what Gregory had told us about Professor Harrison's recent involvement in gambling, something that developed from his initial interest in rooster fighting. "Could gambling debt have caused someone to shoot him?" I asked. "A hit man?"

Bob stirred cream into his fresh cup of coffee. "It could, although murder would satisfy vengeance instead of collecting money. I think the bookie would rather have the money. Have you ever attended a cockfight?"

"No! What makes you ask me that!"

He grinned. "Well, there's a lot to learn there about Professor Harrison's gambling habit. Many different kinds of people attend, even though cockfighting is against the law. Still, it's an ancient tradition, like bullfighting in Spain and Mexico. Your cousin Danny and his father Darryl are in the business of raising roosters; did you know that? Raising roosters is legal, but fighting them is not."

"I didn't know any of that!" I sputtered. "I've barely met Danny and Darryl, even though I've spent a little time with Donny and Aunt Hettie." Suspicion entered my mind. "Hettie's son David lives with her too, but I've only seen him once, at the family meeting."

"He comes and goes. Works on an oil rig in the Gulf of Mexico."

"Oh." I pondered his information. "You certainly know a lot about my family. More than I do in some ways."

"I grew up with them, and you didn't." He grinned again, enjoying his superior status. "Anyway, getting back to the cockfights. Attending them can be dangerous. They're illegal, so no security guards are present. Many people there are only interested in the fights, but there is gambling and drug trade, too. You're right about the possibility that Professor Harrison's murder was generated by his involvement in cockfight gambling. He's been doing that for at least two years, laying his bets with a merciless bookie who is suspected of other murders as well. So far, no proof. Maybe Professor Harrison's death can help us solve this problem."

"Sounds like you already knew more than I told you. How do you know these things?"

He grinned again, this time smugly. "Oh, I have ways. I find things out and take notes." He gave a pointed look to my notebook and grinned at me again.

"I'm a journalist," I protested, rather feebly. "Anyway, I appreciate your information, and I *am* sharing mine with you. Can you tell me if the type of gun used to shoot Professor Harrison has been identified?"

"The bullet was a 9 millimeter, probably from a Glock 17. It doesn't match anything on the computer records at the ballistics office, and we don't have a gun to match it with, so we still don't know who owned the gun, much less who pulled the trigger."

But it wasn't a bullet from Aunt Hettie's Colt .45. The news elated me, but I tried not to show it to Bob. After all, I was still keeping Donny and Aunt Hettie's story in privacy.

Bob must have figured I could tell him something. "Closer to the body, we found something else. A casing from a Colt .45. We didn't find the bullet, but it didn't hit Harrison. It wasn't involved in his death. So I've shared ballistics with you. Do you have anything more to share with me?"

"Aunt Hettie and Donny may have something to tell you," I said carefully. "They're willing to meet with you at your office. How about tomorrow around noon?"

"Sounds fine." No grins; he was serious. "I want to catch whoever shot Thomas Harrison. I doubt it was your Aunt Hettie, but her information could be very helpful." He hesitated then said, "Martha McNair told me Harrison had taken Hettie's address and phone number from the phone book at the library. Maybe he contacted her, and she has something to tell me."

"Martha told me and Janet too." I didn't say anything else.

The waitress arrived with more coffee and a menu for me. For the rest of dinner, we chatted about upcoming April being the wildflower month. When we left the restaurant, Bob followed me home, as if he were a police escort. I waved goodbye to him from my porch, and he zoomed away in his car.

It wasn't even nine o'clock, and I was exuberant about the events of the day. Still full of energy, I approached the stacks of documents at my study's trestle table. In my notebook, I found a page containing information about the grave of Priscilla Gaines in San Antonio and decided to check the post-Civil War census records of DeWitt County and San Antonio to see what I could find.

The Internet plunged me into the ancient documents of Texas. William Gaines turned up in 1880, living in San Antonio with Priscilla Gaines, age sixty-one. She was listed as his mother. He was listed at age thirty-one, and there was another person in the household, Josiah Gaines, listed at age five. Willie had not become married, so perhaps Josiah was a nephew or an orphan he had taken in.

Next, 1890. Priscilla, according to my notes, was buried by then, but William and Josiah remained at the same address. In 1900, Josiah had married, moved to another address, and fathered two children.

I yearned to see photographs of Willie Gaines and his mother Priscilla, who were freed as slaves of the Hargrove family. I wanted to see the family of Josiah Gaines, who was raised by Willie Gaines, and who was born free. I remembered Miranda's comments about the John David and Sarah Elizabeth Hargrove family; she quoted Sarah's letters that mentioned Willie. Sarah said he was courteous

Cemetery Whites

and industrious, and noted that he and his mother were both educated in the Hargrove family.

The Gaines family lived for years in the Ellis Alley area of East San Antonio, an integrated part of town after the Civil War. I wondered what happened to Willie and Josiah and his children, and I hoped things had gone well for them all.

Old newspaper records might have something about the Gaines family—wedding announcements, obituaries—but it was past midnight and I was getting tired. I yawned, clicked off the computer and headed for bed. Tomorrow was already here.

* * *

Having stayed up so late, I slept later than usual, re-setting the alarm clock more than one time. I finally got up, got dressed, fixed toast and coffee for a quick breakfast then drove to Great-Aunt Hettie's house, arriving about nine. Danny and Darryl had already left for the chicken farm, so Donny and Aunt Hettie were the only two who listened to my recital about the ballistics. I repeated what Bob had said. "The bullet removed in autopsy came from a 9 millimeter Glock, even though the casing found near the body came from a Colt .45—yours, of course, Aunt Hettie, although they can't say that until they match its marks with those of your gun. They don't have a gun to match with the Glock bullet, either, but clearly your Colt .45's bullet did not hit Professor Harrison. Somebody else with a Glock gun was there."

Aunt Hettie began to cry, obviously in relief. "I didn't pull that trigger on purpose, but I felt terrible thinking I had killed him even by mistake. Even if he started this mess himself by digging up a grave."

Donny paced around the large front room. "Hot dawg! That's great! Thank you, cousin Caroline. Thank you for your help." He seized my hands with his big paws. "Let's go to the cemetery and see if we can find Grandma's bullet. Maybe it hit a tree limb or a

Connie Knight

tombstone. Then we could bring it to Bob Bennett and let him match it to Grandma's gun. It would give them another proof that she didn't shoot Professor Harrison."

He beamed. "What do you say? Want to come with us?"

"Sure. We need to return before eleven, though, so we can meet Janet here. She'll go with us to Bob Bennett's office. We can tell him what happened and give him the bullet and the Colt .45."

"Oh, it shouldn't take very long," he said. *Optimistic*, I thought.

We piled into my car. I wanted to drive to get a better grip on road directions. We soon pulled up by the cemetery's chain-link fence. To my surprise, another vehicle was already there. It was an old, run-down pickup truck.

The cemetery visitor was easy to see. A tall, thin white-haired old man walked slowly toward the gate. Behind him was a gravestone holding a vase full of bright red roses; the old man carried an empty vase that he must have exchanged.

A guarded look slipped over Aunt Hettie's face. "Hello, Henry," she called as he approached us. We were standing in a group by the gate, and he was getting closer and closer.

"I haven't seen you in such a long time. Remember Donny? And this is my niece Caroline Hargrove Hamilton. She's just moved from Houston to Yorktown, and she's learning all about our family history."

She didn't give him a hug or a kiss, and I could see why. His face was wrinkled and leathery, and twisted into a scowl.

"I read about that black man who got shot here a few days ago," he said abruptly. "I hope you ain't giving him no pauper's grave in our cemetery, Miss Hettie. He shouldn't of been here in the first place. Shouldn't of been digging into Thomas Hargrove's grave. I hope they don't ketch whoever shot him. Good riddance, I say! And I don't want him buried with us, no matter what you might think."

Aunt Hettie was taken aback. I stepped in and said, "Sir, Professor Harrison won't be buried here. His family in San Antonio has a funeral planned for him, and a place in their own family plot, in their church graveyard. And he wasn't a pauper. What made you think he was?"

Henry still scowled. "What was he digging for, if not some kind of treasure?" He put on his dark glasses preparing to drive away in the morning sun. "Though who knows what kind of treasure there might be, other than the second body we don't want anyone to know about."

"He was a history professor," I protested, defending Professor Harrison's unjustified grave digging. "But you're right, he shouldn't have been digging here. He didn't have family permission, and nobody knows what he was looking for."

Henry still scowled. "Hrrumph. Well, have a good day." He nodded good-bye to Hettie and Donny then chugged away in his old truck.

"Well I never!" Hettie said. "That's a cousin I grew up with, but I hardly ever see him anymore. It's a good thing he didn't know Donny and I drove the professor here on that fatal day. He'd probably think I shot him, congratulate me, and spread the false news around town." She looked worse than taken aback—fearful and slightly trembling. "Then I'd be arrested after all."

"Oh, Aunt Hettie, don't be afraid. We're going to find your bullet, remember? Then we'll take it to Bob Bennett and prove your innocence."

Aunt Hettie calmed down. "You're right. Let's go over to where we were standing the other day and see what we can find."

We ended up playing the scene, with me pretending to be Professor Harrison, and Aunt Hettie and Donny standing in their original places. I used my imaginary shovel to swat Aunt Hettie's fantasy pistol out of her hands, and Donny knocked her—with help —to the ground, and we calculated the path of her bullet. It would have headed for a live oak tree near the chain-link fence. We lifted up a thin leafy branch of the tree and, sure enough, hidden beneath it was a splotch of golden metal lodged in the large branch the thin leafy one grew from.

Donny took his pocket knife and carved a plug of wood from the tree branch. The bullet gleamed in the center.

All three of us admired the bullet, then Donny placed it in a plastic bag and I put the bag in my purse. It was time to head back to Hettie's; Janet would be there soon. We climbed into my car and drove to Hettie's house. I found my way pretty well, not asking more than once for directions.

Janet arrived a few minutes after we did. She joined us in the kitchen where Aunt Hettie was brewing a fresh pot of coffee. We had time for a quick cup before driving to Bob Bennett's office.

"I can't have anything right now," Janet said, declining the cup offered to her. "My mouth is thtill numb from the dentist's anesthesia."

"Sounds like you can talk all right. Did you go see Martha McNair? Is she going out with us tonight?"

"Not exactly. She'll meet us at the dance hall near Cuero. She was planning to go there anyway, but she wouldn't say why." She continued to lisp a little as she spoke.

"Oh, well, I guess we'll run into each other. I still want to go, don't you?"

"Sure. Donny, do you want to join us? We're going to hear cousin Lisa's band tonight." Janet's speech was clearing up, but she winced a little as she spoke.

Donny declined; he had other plans. I gulped my coffee and asked him, "Donny, is there a cockfight on Saturday night? One you could take me to?"

He was surprised. "Sure, there's one nearby. Let's make plans later. Isn't it time to go?"

He was right. Everybody climbed into my car, with Janet up front and the other two in the back seat. Janet gave me directions and we parked the car in a few minutes at Bob's office, just before noon.

We entered the little lobby of the small office building, and Bob heard us as we asked the receptionist about him. He welcomed us, took us to a conference room, and listened as Aunt Hettie and Donny described driving Professor Harrison to the Hargrove cemetery after he asked them to. They told Bob how Harrison assembled his collapsible shovel, started digging, and refused to stop in spite of Hettie's request, backed by her gun.

"He started hitting my hands with his shovel, so Donny grabbed for it, but I got knocked down and my gun went off," Hettie said.

I took the bullet in the plastic bag out of my purse. "This is where the bullet went—into a tree limb in the cemetery. It's a Colt .45 bullet, not a 9 millimeter Glock."

"I have my gun here if you want to see it." Meekly, Hettie took her gun out of her purse and handed it over to Bob. I gave him the bullet.

"This should prove Aunt Hettie's innocence. Her bullet didn't hit Professor Harrison. Somebody else must have been there with a Glock handgun."

"I agree." Bob was silent for a minute. "Did Harrison say what he was digging for?" He directed the question to Aunt Hettie and Donny.

"Oh no. It took us by surprise. He was just digging up Thomas Hargrove's grave. I didn't think that was right. That's why I told him to stop, but he didn't listen."

"I agree." Another minute of silence. Another question. "You didn't see the shovel until he produced it to put it together. How did he carry it? In a paper bag? Wrapped in a towel?"

"No, no!" Donny burst out. "It was in a great big briefcase, almost as big as a little suitcase. I forgot about that until now."

"You didn't take the briefcase?"

"No, no. We didn't take anything. When we saw he was dead, we fell to pieces. We ran for our car and drove home."

"We didn't find a briefcase when we arrived there," Bob said. "Somebody else must have taken it, if it wasn't you."

"Whoever shot him! Whoever had the other gun," Donny

crowed in triumph. "Won't that be a way to figure out who it is?"

"It would help, but first we have to find it." Bob rubbed his chin ruefully. "Briefcases these days are common as cow chips. Plenty of them around."

We were quiet. Stumped.

"Um, there's something else," I said. "Suppose it was someone who just happened to be there, someone who hates black people and just took advantage of the chance to shoot him?" I told Bob about cousin Henry's point of view. "Maybe someone like him shot Harrison, and took the briefcase along for no particular reason."

"Could be, but we haven't found anything pointing us to any particular person who happened to be out in the middle of the county at just the right time to pull a gun and shoot."

"Well—sometimes things happen even if they're not planned."

Bob grinned. "Yes, but the problem is still difficult to solve. No suspect, no motive, no guns to track down the owner. The information you just gave me about Harrison's request for a ride, and his big briefcase that has disappeared, is fresh. We'll see if we can find the briefcase. Maybe somebody in town is carrying it around."

He stood up and so did we, preparing to leave the conference room. "Thank you for telling me about your encounter with Professor Harrison," he told Aunt Hettie and Donny. "Thanks for the gun and the bullet, too, and especially for the new clue about the briefcase."

We piled back into my car and I drove us to Aunt Hettie's. Janet decided to go straight home to relax and recover from her dental work. She wanted to be in good shape for going to hear Lisa's band tonight.

I followed Donny into the house and we made plans for Saturday.

"I can pick you up about five o'clock, and we can stop at Danny's chicken farm to take a look at the roosters he and Daddy are raising. Then we'll move on until we get to the rooster fight

Cemetery Whites

arena. It's not too far away. We'll be kind of early, but I'd rather do that and leave early too, if you don't mind. Things get pretty het up sometimes late at night."

"Early's fine with me," I said. "Thanks for everything, Donny. I'll see you tomorrow at five."

"That's a deal." We shook hands on it, he walked me to the front door, and I drove on home. Janet's idea of an afternoon rest seemed like a good one to me.

Connie Knight

CHAPTER SEVEN
Friday, March 19, 2010

On my way home from Aunt Hettie's house, I stopped at Casa Rosa for a cup of coffee and a bite to eat. It was almost two o'clock and high time for lunch. Someone had left a copy of the Yorktown *Chronicle*, a twice-weekly newspaper, on my table. It was an old issue from Wednesday, the paper containing the article about the Sutton-Taylor Feud.

I sipped my coffee and flipped through the paper. The feud article appeared on the front page of the Lifestyle section. It was easy to find. I re-read it twice, pondering the stories about the Hargroves, James Jamison, and Professor Harrison. A columnist wrote the feud article; he put forth opinions, conjectures, points of view. His ideas might be likely but they were not rock-solid data. Nothing was proven.

Well, so what? The writer presented his story as a rumor. Some solid things, like Jamison's gold watch and gun, were found near the Hargrove homestead, but most of the story was given as a possibility.

I ate my order of enchiladas and thought about the things I wrote working in public relations. My press releases and newsletter articles presented positive information about the museum where I worked. Before that, in my first work as a journalist, I had written feature articles for a newspaper and regional magazines.

Maybe I would enjoy writing again. I'd like to write about the things I'm finding out. History, current events, interviews with various people. Right now, I can think of a dozen articles in progress from my history research and interviews—though none of them are ready to write about yet.

I paid my bill, got into my car, and switched on the engine. Which way to go? Home, or downtown?

I chose downtown. Five minutes later I was in the lobby of the Yorktown *Chronicle*, asking to see the editor.

Fifteen minutes later, I left the office with an assignment. I'd write a column about moving from Houston to Yorktown, reuniting with my family. Barry Wilson, the editor, liked that idea. A trend was developing, he said, of baby-boom retirees moving back home instead of staying in the cities where they'd gone in their youth to attend college and find jobs.

I'd write the article and he'd review it. Payment to be discussed. Possible articles on the Harrison death, the rooster fight business, the Hargrove family history, the Sutton-Taylor Feud—these could be considered later, but not yet. Too many things were still up in the air.

At home, I lay down on my living room's cushiony sofa and flipped on the TV. Janet and Jordan would pick me up at six-thirty then we'd drive to Billie's Bar-B-Que in Cuero for dinner and dancing. Lisa Hargrove and Martha McNair were expecting our arrival. I wanted to be refreshed and relaxed for the evening.

* * *

When Janet and Jordon pulled up in the maroon sedan, I had changed into black silk slacks with a dark red low-cut blouse and a black silk shawl. A little too dressy, I realized, when I saw Jordan, still wearing his work clothes—khaki pants and a plaid shirt—and Janet, in a denim skirt and cotton blouse.

"Should I change my clothes?" I asked, opening the car's back door.

"No, no. You look great." Janet said it, and Jordan smiled approvingly too.

I climbed into the back seat and buckled the seat belt. "If it's okay with you, it's okay with me," I said. "I haven't been to Billie's Bar-B-Que yet, and I didn't know quite what to wear."

Conversation shifted from clothes to careers as I told them about my brand-new journalism assignment. "A new job!" Janet said, sounding impressed. "Will you make a lot of money?"

I laughed. "Probably not. Payment hasn't been discussed. Anyway, it's not a full-time job, just a free-lance column now and then."

"When I write things down at work, I have to think them out first," Jordan said. "Sometimes things shift around, or new thoughts develop. Does that happen with you?"

"Oh yes. Keeping a journal makes that happen, too. I used to do that, and I should resume that habit. It might help me organize my new life here in Yorktown. Sometimes you understand things better when you've written them down."

I was wringing my hands and didn't know it, but Janet looked back at me and saw it. "Oh, Carrie," she said. "You're doing very well with making a space for yourself in Yorktown. You've got detective work, a newspaper job, and family history as a hobby. You're making friends, too—me and Jordan, Martha McNair, Bob Bennett, Aunt Hettie and Donny. Maury and Elizabeth and Uncle Cotton are glad to see you here, too. And you're certainly finding ways to spend your time. The two of us are busy as bees. That's more than I used to do on my own before you moved here."

"She's right," said Jordan.

My emotional distress embarrassed me. I kept a journal before Craig died, and after his death, I set it aside. I didn't want to write about things that are so painful. Only lately have I been accepting the fact of his loss, and I didn't discuss it with anyone. Maybe keeping a journal would help me come to terms with the past as well as organize the future.

"I don't mean to seem upset," I said to Janet and Jordan. "I like living in Yorktown, but my life is changing in many ways. Look, let's have a good time tonight. I want to hear Lisa's band, and try Billie's barbecue. I've heard it's delicious."

"Do you shoot pool?" Jordan asked.

"Yes, I do. That's something I learned in college. Not as a class, exactly. Why are you asking?"

"Oh, I play a little. There's a separate room at Billie's with a few pool tables. Bands don't play there every night, so shooting pool is kind of like a dessert on some evenings."

"We'll try it out." The thought was cheery and I laughed. During the rest of the trip, we talked about Lisa's band and others in the area.

"If you like music so much, you ought to come to church with us Sunday mornings," Janet said. "Maybe you could sing in the choir like Martha McNair."

I used to sing solos in my Houston church, but I didn't want to discuss that now. We had reached Billie's Bar-B-Que and Jordan was parking the car.

"I'll go to church with you on Sunday," I told Janet. "But I might keep out of choir practice for the time being."

Billie's occupied an old Victorian two-story house on the edge of town. On the side of the building, there was plenty of room to park, and in the pretty backyard there was space for wedding receptions and other celebrations. Large oak trees in the front yard framed the view of the building itself, sitting at the end of a long pathway.

Once inside, we found ourselves in a large room with a bar on one side and a small-sized dance floor with a stage for the band at the far end of the room. There were wood-paneled walls, ceiling fans, lots of square wooden tables. Some had already been pushed together to make places for eight or twelve people. Reservation cards sat in the center of large tables and small ones too. We were early, but additional groups were filtering in as we took our seats and settled down.

The band was on stage, setting up their equipment. Lisa, I

knew, played rhythm guitar and her boyfriend Richard played lead. There was someone else with a bass, someone with a banjo, and someone with a fiddle and a mandolin. They were plugging in their microphones and amplifiers, putting some chairs onstage, and placing stands to hold the instruments when they were not in use.

"Testing, testing," Lisa said, speaking into her microphone. She made a few adjustments and everything was done. She looked at the restaurant tables, assessing the night's attendance. The crowd was building up; waiters and waitresses were busy bringing customers beer and drinks, taking their barbecue orders. When she looked at our table, Lisa's face lighted up, and she left the stage and walked toward us. We had placed our orders, but so far only drinks had been delivered.

Lisa gave Janet and Jordan each a hug and a kiss, then leaned over the table to welcome me. "I remember you from the family meeting a few days ago. Are you finding anything out about the murder?"

"Just a bit," I responded. "Janet and I are both working on the project. We ought to file a report with cousin David, since he was in charge of the meeting when I volunteered."

"I'd like to know who did such a thing in our family cemetery," Lisa said. "Please let me know when you find anything out."

Lisa looked glamorous. A cowboy hat, tilted back on her head, topped her long, blond, curly hair. Her skin was smooth, and her makeup skillfully applied. She wore a black silky rodeo shirt, with red roses embroidered on the shoulders and ivory fringes falling from the sleeves. Black denim jeans and red leather boots completed the outfit. All the other band members wore similar clothes, but not as silky and snazzy as hers.

"Are you playing here every Friday night now?" Jordan asked her.

"Here every Friday and other places most Saturday nights. There's a schedule on our website. Look under Oak Creek Bluegrass Band."

Cemetery Whites

"We will. We ought to come hear you more often."

Lisa laughed as she squeezed Jordan's shoulder. "Thanks. It's nice to see you here. Look, you have a friend headed your way."

She nodded her head toward the door, and we saw Martha McNair threading her way toward our table. She smiled and waved at us, and Jordan stood up and pulled a chair away from the table to seat her when she arrived.

"Thank you, Jordan." Martha sat down and said hello. A chorus of greetings burst forth from everyone at the table. Lisa said, "Hi, Martha. Remember me? My band played at your library one afternoon last year. We performed some cowboy songs for the elementary and junior high school students. Remember?"

"*Come along boys and listen to my tale, I'll tell you 'bout my troubles on the Old Chisholm Trail.*" Martha sang the first two lines of the song that had opened the program. "I remember your band very well. Haven't any of the teachers asked you to repeat the performance this year?"

"No, I haven't heard from anyone. If you want to organize something with the schools for an afternoon, I'm sure we could find time for it."

"I'll do that on Monday, and call you that afternoon. Thanks for volunteering! We'll work something out."

Lisa departed, going to another table to chat with other band fans. The waiter delivered baskets of bread and took Martha's order for a barbecue plate. "Someone else will be here soon," she told the waiter. He set napkins and flatware down for a table setting next to Martha's place.

Our table for six would be almost full, I thought. "Who's joining us?" I asked Martha. Janet, I could tell, was extremely interested in the answer.

"You'll meet my fiancé, Allen Boyce. He works here in Cuero. He's an architect for a firm that's renovating historical buildings in this area. He works on houses and commercial buildings, too."

"So that's why you moved from San Antonio to Yorktown.

You're engaged to be married!"

"That's part of it." Martha smiled. Her gold earrings glittered in the dim light thrown by the table lamps. "The library job in Yorktown was the only one open in this area. Anyway, I like it. I plan to keep working there even after Allen and I marry next fall."

"What's the date?" Janet asked, but Martha didn't hear her. "Allen!" she called, and waved to a tall, handsome black man standing near the front door, scanning the nearly-full room in search of Martha McNair. He saw her waving, smiled back, and threaded his way through the crowded room toward our table.

"Hello, hello," he said when he reached us. All of us introduced ourselves, and Allen sat down next to Martha. They were obviously happy to see each other. Allen ordered a drink and a barbecue plate, which arrived with ours just as the band took the stage and started its first set of music.

We ate our dinner, listened to the music, and joined the audience in applause. Lisa's band was excellent, I thought. Close your eyes and it sounded like a Grammy-winning CD. Lisa's voice, backed by others, sounded like Dolly Parton or Patsy Cline. She was a soprano with great control over the phrasing of each line she sang, and the emotional heights of heartache, loneliness, joy, or love. In the break of each song, the banjo, the fiddle, the lead guitar would take over for a dazzling instrumental rendition of Lisa's lyrics.

Some couples finished their dinners before we did. They left their tables and went to the dance floor, swirling around under the chandelier lights. For the last song of the set, Allen and Martha joined the dancers and circled the dance floor gracefully. Good dancers, they seemed to me. Allen was taller than Martha, and she tilted her head back to look into his dark brown eyes. She smiled as she talked to him, and he smiled back while he listened to her attentively.

They returned to the table and Janet started a conversation about the upcoming wedding. Jordan looked at me and said, "Still want to shoot some pool?" I'd forgotten about that, but the suggestion was enticing.

"Sure. Where do we go from here?"

A door near the stage led to another large room. There were four pool tables, a rack of pool cues, powdery chalk for your hands, and cubes of blue chalk for the cue tips.

We rolled cue sticks on the pool tables, each of us searching for one that was well-tipped, straight, and just the right weight. Jordan put quarters into the pool table's slots, and the balls rumbled out. He arranged them—solids and stripes—into the triangular rack at one end of the table.

"You break 'em," he told me.

I gave the white cue ball the strongest shot I could muster, aiming at the side of the triangle of solids and stripes.

I was lucky. Hadn't played pool in several years, but my shot successfully broke up the balls, scattered them over the table, and even sank two striped balls into the table's pockets.

"Hot dawg!" Jordan exclaimed, and I couldn't help grinning ear to ear.

"Stripes," I said, and proceeded to sink another three striped balls before losing my turn to Jordan.

He had seven solid balls to sink before putting the eight ball into a specified pocket, but with five stripes out of the way, his pathways were pretty clear. He ran five, missed one, and the turn became mine.

One stripe was close to a corner pocket, and I nudged it in without sinking the cue ball too. The other stripe was in the middle of the table, and the eight-ball sat on the perilous edge of a side pocket. If you accidentally pocket the eight-ball before you've finished with your solids or stripes, you lose.

The obvious shot to try would be difficult to make. I wanted the cue ball to knock the stripe into a corner pocket then roll back into the middle of the table where it could put the eight-ball into the side pocket. Danger: it might hit the eight-ball accidentally and knock it into the pocket first, and I'd lose the game.

Jordan grinned at me and I smiled back. "Corner pocket for the stripe," I said, then leaned over and made it happen.

"Whoo!" I crowed. "I can't believe it." The cue ball had rolled into the middle of the table, almost behind the eight-ball. An easy hit.

But there was a problem: if the cue ball followed the eight-ball into the side pocket, I'd lose. There were options for the final shot. Might work, or might not.

I smiled at Jordan again. "Eight-ball in the side pocket," I said, and hit the cue ball with upper right English. It hit the eight-ball, which took a curvy path that put it into the side pocket, but the cue ball rolled on until it hit the table's side rail and stopped.

I'd won! I looked at Jordan with some chagrin, which wasn't necessary. Jordan was laughing with delight. He reached out and gave me a hug. "Why didn't you tell me you're so good at this! I might have got somebody to bet on me, and I'd have bet on you."

"Well, you might have lost," I told him. "I haven't played in a long time. These shots really were lucky."

We played another couple of games then heard the band begin to play. They were back on stage, so we hung up our cue sticks and went back to the table.

Allen and Martha were back on the dance floor, and the table's empty chair—number six—had been filled. Bob Bennett, in civilian clothes instead of his constable uniform, stood up and pulled my chair out for me.

I was glad to see him. I gave him a dazzling smile.

He grinned back at me.

"Bob, what brings you here tonight? Did someone tell you we'd be here?"

He glanced at Janet, who began to blush. Jordan, once again sitting beside her, saw her blush and began to laugh. "Aha! Dirt shows up on the cleanest cotton. You told Bob we'd be here, didn't you? Why didn't you just invite him? He could have ridden with us."

Cemetery Whites

"Actually, she did, but I couldn't leave Yorktown as soon as y'all did. I had some work to finish, so I drove over in my own car."

"It's nice to see you, Bob," I told him, making it clear he was welcome. Of course, he was an old friend of Jordan's, so why wouldn't he join us? Why Janet had kept his invitation secret was another issue, but not important. I rather enjoyed the surprise of Bob's sudden appearance.

I told him about the game of pool Jordan and I had played. "I won the first one, and another one later on. I haven't played in years. I must be recovering former abilities, like shooting pool, doing research, writing newspaper articles. Did anyone tell you about that? I'll be working free-lance for the Yorktown *Chronicle*. I can hardly wait to see my name in print once again."

Bob was careful in phrasing his question. "Are you planning to write an article on cockfighting, by any chance?"

"Yes, I am, although it won't be the first one. Now who told you about that?"

"Someone who's concerned about your safety."

"Is a rooster fight raid planned for tomorrow? Is a drug gang coming in and taking over? What's going on?"

"Now, now," Bob said to soothe me. "It's not that bad. Just be cautious in who you talk to, what you say. I can't be there, but let Donny lead the way. He and Danny and Darryl are well-known and respected. Let it be clear that you are with them, and you will be safe."

"I might be safe anyhow, wouldn't I?"

"Maybe, but as I said before, there are no law officers or security guards at this illegal activity. Just be careful. Why are you going there anyway?"

We re-hashed the possibility that gambling debt caused Professor Harrison's death. "I'm not exactly going undercover," I said. "Learning about the family I'm returning to—I guess that's what interests me. If I find out anything connected to the murder, I'll let you know. You can bust the killer, and I'll stay out of the way."

It was a deal; we shook hands on it. Jordan and Janet returned to the table; so did Allen and Martha. The conversation topic changed, the band took a break, and Jordan took Janet to play a game of pool.

Allen, it turned out, had moved to Cuero about two years ago, when a large church in another city was being restored. He came to like living in the country, and, when the church was done, signed up for other projects in the area, rather than moving back to San Antonio.

"Do you have family here?" I asked.

"No, not that I'm aware of. We're from San Antonio, at least back to my grandparents. I've never done any family tree research, although the work I'm doing has sparked my interest in Texas history generally. Martha finds Texana books for me at the library now and then."

"We met in San Antonio," Martha chimed in. "I was getting ready to retire when Allen was assigned here. So I looked for a second job, and found one in Yorktown. I like it here too, and now that we're engaged, we're looking for a house around here—maybe one to restore."

"Would a farmhouse interest you?" Bob asked. "There's one on the road where I live. It's been for sale for a while. The ranch it belonged to has already sold, but the house comes with a few acres, and there's a long driveway from the house to the road. The Schuler family lived there until five years ago. You might want to remodel it, but it's in basically good shape. Not falling apart."

Martha and Allen seemed interested. "We've been looking in the towns so far, but a farmhouse—we should take a look."

Bob wrote down the real estate agent's name and the house address and gave it to Allen. Jordan and Janet returned to the table; Lisa's band returned to the stage, and the music sent Martha and Allen back to the dance floor. At the table, conversation stopped. We listened to the band's country music.

Cemetery Whites

Bob moved his chair a little closer to mine. "Going to church with Janet on Sunday?" he asked, leaning over so I could hear him as well as the music.

I nodded. "First time. I'm checking it out."

"I'll see you there then," he said.

"Are you leaving now?"

"Oh, no. I'm staying. But you're occupied with the rooster fights tomorrow, so I won't see you until Sunday morning. Can I take you to lunch after the service?"

His invitation surprised me. He was still leaning toward me, smiling, waiting for a reply.

"Sure," I said. "That will be nice. We'll get together again on Sunday morning. You'll have to take me home after lunch, though, because I'm riding to church with Janet and Jordan."

Bob's smile grew into a grin, and he draped one arm on the back of my chair. For the rest of the evening, we sat like that, leaning slightly into each other, smiling, and listening to music.

73

CHAPTER EIGHT
Saturday, March 20, 2010

"Usually I ride my Harley-Davidson, but I didn't think you'd like that, so I borrowed Grandma's car." Donny carefully pulled the Oldsmobile onto the highway and stayed in the right-hand, slow lane.

I remembered three motorcycles parked side by side at the family meeting Wednesday night. "Do Darryl and Danny have motorcycles too?"

"Oh, yeah. Theirs are nicer and newer than mine, though. They make money from the rooster farm, but I'm not working at a job. I just stay home to work on the farm and take care of Grandma. She don't like to admit it, but sometimes she needs a little help."

Donny's candid statement lacked any rancor, and I found it quite endearing. "Aunt Hettie must be grateful for your help. I guess she's not as independent as she used to be, now that she's in her eighties."

Donny snorted. "Independent as a hog on ice. It's real hard for her to ask for help, and if I'm not around, sometimes she'll get herself into trouble. She'll pick up things that are too heavy and might make her fall down, or she'll open a gate to let out a cow that walks faster than she can. When I'm home, I just step in and do those things for her. There's still plenty that she can do, and it's fine with me for her to do all that. We split chores in a way. She does the light work, and I do the rest. And she still owns a car. She has a driver's license, too. She drives this Oldsmobile to town and does her own grocery shopping, then comes home and cooks."

He turned the Oldsmobile onto an old dirt road. "This will get us to the rooster farm. It's a couple miles down the road."

The road was shaded by tall oak trees growing on each side. Eventually we turned onto a dirt driveway that led to a small white farmhouse. You couldn't see it from the road because of the trees, but around the house the land had been cleared for farming. A chain-link fence enclosed a yard around the house, and a few rose bushes were blooming on each side of the front porch.

Donny parked the car in front of the house. From its position, I could see a field of roosters some distance from the right-hand side of the house. The long, rectangular field was immaculately maintained. A bright green grass covered the soil, forming a background for a number of plywood A-frame rooster shelters. They were arranged in a regular pattern. Each shelter covered a single-chicken feeder and container of water. In front of the shelter, a metal bar driven into the ground anchored a tether attached to a beautiful, brightly colored rooster. The cocks shared the field, but couldn't reach each other and start a fight.

The view mesmerized me. The green grass formed a shimmering background, the golden plywood A-frames created a pattern, and the colorful roosters strutted beside the frames. The field looked like a beautiful quilt with a green background and a geometrical pattern formed by A-frames and gamecocks.

Donny waited patiently for my return to reality. "Something to look at, ain't it?" he commented, as I began to regain my normal senses.

"They're gorgeous," I said.

"Tell that to Daddy and Danny. They'll be glad to hear it."

The two gamefowl breeders were now standing on the front porch, waiting for us to come forward. I collected my purse, portfolio, pen and paper, and followed Donny through the front yard.

Darryl looked very much like an older version of his sons Donny and Danny. He was tall and muscular, just like the twins, but his face was creased, his hairline receded, and his blond hair was streaked with gray. Danny and Donny were absolutely identical twins. If they had dressed in the same clothing, it would have been impossible to tell them apart.

Donny and I climbed the steps to the porch, and everyone began to say hello to everyone else. "Daddy, you remember Caroline from the family meeting at Uncle Cotton's, don't you?" Donny said.

"I remember seeing her there," Darryl said. "I didn't get to say hello, though. We were across the room."

"We howdied, but we ain't shook," said Danny. He and his father were both smiling at Donny and me. He held his hand out, and so did his father, to shake my hand and welcome me.

They led us into the small house, where a table in the front room was set with plates and glasses. "We ought to have a bite to eat before we leave." Darryl brought in a pitcher of sweet iced tea and a plate of cornbread. Danny followed with a bowl of salad and another bowl of pinto beans. The beans smelled good, and suddenly I felt hungry.

We filled our plates, and I listened as the men talked. Someone had already come by with a truck filled with cages, and had bought a dozen roosters to take to the cockfight tonight.

"They bought roosters instead of raising their own?" I wanted to understand the protocol.

"Most raise their own, but some don't. We raise good gamecocks, and have several customers who buy them from us. They hope to make their money back, and then some. I guess it works for them, because they keep on coming back."

"We ought to place bets on our roosters sometimes, Daddy," Danny said.

"Oh, no, we don't. Let other people do that. The quickest way to double your money is to fold it over and put it back into your pocket. Always better than betting."

Donny and Danny had heard Darryl say that before. They joined him in reciting the practical advice about making investments.

"If you're not putting your own roosters in the fight, and you're not placing bets, why are you going?" Their plans bewildered me.

Danny explained, "It's kind of like going to a wrestling match, or a bull fight in Mexico. It's something special to see."

Darryl added, "Besides, we go down to the cockpit and help with getting our gamecocks ready for the pit. We give support to our customers that way.

"I see." My reason for attending the rooster fight had to do with tracking the path of Professor Harrison rather than rooting for any rooster to win. It was a struggle to understand their reasons, except Donny, who was going because I asked him to take me.

Danny cleared the dishes from the table. I could sense his growing excitement. It was time to drive to the cockfight.

Donny and I were ready to drive there, too. "We'll see you there later," Donny said.

"Thanks for dinner," I said, and meant it. "Thanks for explaining things to me, too."

Back in the Oldsmobile, we turned the car and headed back for the highway. We were still driving at a moderate speed. "It'll take us about an hour to get there."

We reached the arena a little after seven o'clock. A dirt road led off the highway and wound around. Donny turned onto a long driveway and ended up in a grassy parking area. He parked the car near the driveway, in a place that promised quick exit. We'd probably leave for home earlier than most, and we didn't want to be blocked in.

I gathered my purse and paper pad with pen, finding room in the purse for the pen and paper. I didn't want to look like a journalist at the cockfight. In fact, I'd followed Janet's advice in dressing for the evening. Blue jeans, cotton shirt, a leather jacket borrowed from Janet, and my own cowboy boots. They were several years old but felt like new; I'd only worn them before to Houston's annual livestock show and rodeo. Donny's everyday boots were

Connie Knight

scuffed and creased, but probably much more comfortable than mine.

I followed him out of the parking lot, onto a path leading to a barn-like building with an open door. It was early, but people were starting to filter in. Bleacher seats circled the cock pit, with an area for cockers and their cages of roosters and bags of equipment. Bright lights hung from the ceiling beams, especially lighting the cock pit. This must be a high-level place, I thought. On one end of the building, there was a cart selling sausage on a stick and French fries. Next to it, another cart sold cans of beer and bottles of soda water.

Donny led us to a place to sit. From it, I had a good view of the cock pit. I could see Darryl and Danny, each holding a gamecock and talking to a well-dressed man who must have been one of their customers. He looked like the owner of the roosters.

Donny nudged me and nodded in a different direction. "Gambling," he whispered. The group of men re-shaped themselves in my eyes. One had a notebook and was writing things down. Men approached him, chatted for a minute and then ambled away. The growing crowd consisted more of men than women. Then it struck me that one of the men in the crowd of bettors looked a lot like Professor Harrison's teaching assistant, Gregory Jackson.

Ardently I wished for my birdwatcher's binoculars, which I hadn't thought of bringing to the rooster fight. They would have helped me ascertain the identity of the skinny young man with straight blond hair. Was he really Gregory Jackson? If so, was he placing his bets with the same bookie who—according to what Gregory had said in San Antonio—might have sent a hit man after Professor Harrison?

Jackson, in a minute, was talking to the bookie, apparently placing his bet. Then he walked away, heading for the bleachers. He was alone, walking slowly, swigging now and then from a can of beer carried in his hand.

Just then the rooster fights began. Down in the pit, far enough

Cemetery Whites

away I couldn't see anything in detail, two roosters were released and flew into each other's space. Their fight was violent, savage, and quick. One of them slashed the other one's chest with sharp knives tied to the spurs on its feet. One cock won; the other one died. Both were removed from the pit.

Donny watched the fight pensively. "You don't like this, do you?" I asked him.

"Not really," he admitted. "I take care of our cows and chickens at home, and that doesn't include anything to do with training them to fight. I don't see why it's against the law, though. People have been doing this for hundreds of years."

To my surprise, I agreed with him. Fighting each other was genetic in the gamecocks, just as it is in many animals. Television shows and films display mountain goats and rams, deer, elks, wild horses, all fighting over territory or a female, sometimes to the point that one is left dying while the other one wins. Then there are predatory animals—owls, hawks, eagles, snakes, cougars, tigers, lions—who are not vegetarian. They hunt, kill, and eat their prey— bugs, mice, frogs, rabbits. If the predators are large animals, their prey may be large, too. Deer, zebras, sheep, goats, sometimes human beings.

Organizations to prevent cruelty to animals have backed laws preventing cockfighting, but it goes on anyway around the world. Bullfighting continues in Mexico and Spain. So does wrestling and boxing among human beings. That, I don't like, and I don't like dog fighting either. Wrestlers, boxers, and pit bulls, for example, have higher intelligence and better personalities than gamecocks. Pit bulls can be good pets unless they are trained to fight. They aren't vicious fighters unless they've been trained to be that way.

Another rooster fight ended, and my thoughts returned to Gregory Jackson. He had found a place to sit, not too far away, and there was a vacant seat next to him.

"Donny, I'll be back in a few minutes. I'm going to talk to that man." I pointed Jackson out so Donny would know where I would go. He nodded, and I knew he'd watch me while I was gone.

I threaded my way through the crowd of rooster fight fans, most of them holding a beer, and reached Gregory Jackson in a few minutes. He was sitting alone, swigging his beer, and looking glum. I tapped his shoulder and worked up a wide smile. He was startled by my tap, jumped, and turned toward me with a scowl on his face.

I kept on smiling. "Remember me? I met you at Professor Harrison's house in San Antonio a few days ago."

His scowl diminished. "Caroline Hamilton, isn't it? I remember you and your cousin Janet. Is she here tonight too?"

"No, I'm here with another cousin, Donny Harrell." I pointed to Donny, who smiled and waved.

Gregory's scowl disappeared and turned into curiosity. "I used to come here with Professor Harrison, and I've met him before. I thought his name was Danny, not Donny. He raises roosters and usually sits down in the cockpit, like a football coach getting his players ready to fight."

I laughed. "There is a Danny in the cockpit." I pointed him out. "Over there, see? Danny and Donny are identical twins, but Danny is the one who raises roosters, along with their father Darryl."

"For God's sake! I never knew that. Never saw them together." His mouth clamped shut and the scowl returned as he thought something over.

"One of them used to give betting tips to the professor. Sometimes they worked out, sometimes they didn't. Maybe sometimes it was Donny and sometimes Danny? One was usually right, the other one wrong?"

My smile faded away. "I doubt it. Donny doesn't usually go to the fights, but Danny always does. He must have given all the tips, but they couldn't always be right. I don't think the fights are fixed. I've heard it's unusual for a rooster to win more than two or three fights before losing the next one. I wouldn't know which one to bet on. Would you? Didn't I see you in the crowd of bettors earlier tonight?"

Cemetery Whites

Gregory sighed. "You're right. I placed a few bets. So far I'm breaking even. It's better than losing, and anyway my bets are small. I can't afford gambling with hundreds of dollars like the professor."

"Why are you placing bets at all, when it caused such disaster for the professor?"

"I'm not acting like he did. I'd drive him down here, he'd drink a few beers, and he'd start flying high as a kite. He gambled much more money than he should have. If he won, he'd take the money and bet it again. I don't know why in the world he got so involved with this, except it seemed to have something to do with that history research project of mine. You know, my dissertation."

He looked at me, and I nodded. "I remember."

"Professor Harrison's own family history was included in the project, and I admit doing some extra work about it because of him. I told you about it, didn't I? I researched the changes in the lives of former slaves in this area following the Civil War. The professor's ancestors moved to San Antonio and did very well. They became a large, prosperous family."

"The professor did very well, except for gambling. Didn't you tell me he might have been shot by a gambling cartel's hit man?"

"Shh! Shh!" Gregory's face took on a stricken look. "Don't let anybody hear you say I said that."

"Okay. I won't repeat it." I spoke in a quiet voice, but he seemed to hear me. "Are things working out okay for you?" I asked, to change the subject.

"Oh, pretty good. It's coming along. My dissertation is almost done, and I'll still be employed as a teaching assistant, just for a different professor. I'm still living in the garage apartment, too."

"Will you attend Professor Harrison's funeral on Monday?"

"Is it on Monday? For God's sake, Estelle Shawn didn't let me know!"

"It was in the San Antonio *Express-News* yesterday in his obituary." I'd already heard about it from Bob Bennett, but I had seen it in the Friday paper as well. "Janet and I plan to attend.

Connie Knight

Maybe we'll see you there?"

I stood up. We were between cockfights and I wanted to work my way through the crowd back to Donny.

"I'll be there. I wasn't invited, but I guess they won't kick me out. Listen, thanks for mentioning the funeral. I would have regretted missing it."

"See you there." I pushed my way back to the bleacher where Donny was sitting.

We watched a few more rooster fights then decided to drive on home. It was after nine o'clock—late enough for Donny and for me, too. We headed out of the bleachers, and walked toward the food stand. Donny wanted some sausage on a stick. He stood in line, and I walked over to the top row of the bleacher seats. I stood there, watching the roosters fight, waiting for Donny.

I didn't see the bookie leave his post and walk over to me. "Wanna place a bet, girlie?" he said to me. His voice and presence startled me and made me jump. I turned around to see him. He was a rotund man with thinning hair. A smile was pasted on his face, but his eyes were hard and cold.

"Ha ha," he said. "I didn't mean to scare you. I was making a joke."

I gathered my wits to answer him. "Do I know you?"

"My name is Paul, and I'm in charge of the gambling here. Other places, too. I know who you are, and I've heard about you. You're trying to find whoever killed Professor Harrison, who was so deep in gambling debt. Well, I'm here to tell you, it's true about the debt, but it ain't true about me hiring a hit man to take him out. Why would I do that? Now that he's dead, I've lost my chance of ever collecting that money."

"Makes sense." Agreement seemed necessary.

"Hah!" he said. "Keep that in mind when you see Bob Bennett." He paused a moment. "One more thing I'd appreciate. When you write articles for the newspaper, don't write about rooster fights and gambling. Everybody already knows everything, but it's better to keep it private. Know what I mean?"

"I wasn't planning to write anything about you, or anything about gambling," I protested.

"Just keep it in mind," he said, and walked off. He must have seen Donny heading toward me. I saw him, too, when I turned around because of Paul's departure.

"Something going on?" Donny asked.

"Nothing major." I recounted Paul's speech as we walked away from the bleachers. "It was Gregory Jackson who told me Harrison might have been shot by a bookie's hit man, and I saw him talking to Paul earlier tonight. I suppose he could have warned Paul about me and my journalism, though I don't see why."

"Making points with Paul. He's playing it both ways," Donny said. "Unless Daddy or Danny said something. They know about your journalism, and they know Paul, too, even though they don't gamble. They wouldn't want a newspaper article that would cause any trouble for the business of rooster fights."

"That's not very nice. That really hurts my feelings."

"Daddy and Danny wouldn't have wanted Paul to be so bossy. I think he was like that because he wants you to believe he didn't have anything to do with the professor's murder. He wants you to leave him alone, and leave him out of the newspaper."

"Do you think Paul's innocent? Of the murder, I mean."

By now we were walking in the parking lot, near the Oldsmobile, and could speak more freely than in the crowd. Still, Donny spoke in a low voice. "Oh, probably. Don't know either way for sure, do we?"

I had to agree. "No. It's hard to come up with a culprit. There aren't many clues. Bob's office hasn't identified the owner of the gun, and they haven't located the briefcase."

Donny opened the car door for me, and I settled in. Soon we were back on the road home. We traveled in silence, both of us thinking of Professor Harrison's death.

We finally parked in front of my house. The porch light was on, and Donny walked me up to the front door. I unlocked it and flipped on the living room light.

"Thank you for your help, Donny," I said. "I doubt I could have located that place on my own, much less made it through the night so easily."

"Oh, you're welcome. You and Janet come and visit me and Grandma now and then, and let me know if I can help you out with anything."

"I will. I really appreciate your offer."

Donny smiled. "That's what families are for." He turned and walked back to the Oldsmobile, but waited until I stepped into the house before he switched his engine on.

He headed down the street, and I headed into my kitchen. It was time for a bedtime snack. I walked in the dark to the kitchen sink, where there was a switch to turn on the light.

Looking out the kitchen window, I saw something that frightened me. My hand froze, and I stayed in the dark. Someone had parked a car in my backyard driveway. The entrance to the driveway came from the side street; you couldn't see it from the front where Donny had dropped me off.

My eyes got used to the dark, and I thought I could see someone sitting in the driver's seat. The car was small, but I couldn't see the license plates, or tell the make or model of the vehicle either.

A minute ticked by. Then the car's engine started. No headlights flipped on, but the car backed out of my driveway, made a turn, and headed down the side street. A block away, the headlights appeared and the car's speed picked up. It made a right turn and sped out of sight.

My heart hammered and my hand trembled. I went through my house, room by room, flicked on the lights, checked the closets, made sure the back door and all the windows were locked. I checked my study. My stacks of papers were in order; nothing had been touched.

Cemetery Whites

Fury overcame my fear. Who had parked in my driveway? Why? Did someone feel threatened by my investigation of the murder? If so, someone thought I knew more than I really did.

I turned on my security alarm, then called the constable's office and reported the incident. The night shift constable agreed to patrol my neighborhood through the night.

I wasn't hungry anymore. Instead of a snack, I took a long, hot, soaking bath. All the tension slowly faded away. After midnight, I went to bed. I set the alarm clock first, so I'd wake up in plenty of time to go to church in the morning.

CHAPTER NINE
Sunday, March 21, 2010

The church service started at eleven o'clock, so I slept late to recover from the cockfight I'd attended, and the fright from the mysterious car at my house Saturday night. My alarm clock went off at eight o'clock in the morning, giving me time to brew a cup of coffee and toast an English muffin. Nothing refreshes me like a good night's sleep and a leisurely breakfast in the morning.

Jordan and Janet picked me up at ten-thirty, and I rode in the back seat with their sons Christopher and Kenny. Christopher would be driving back to Texas A&M in the evening, so Janet would make his favorite Sunday dinner when the church service was over.

Christopher was growing up and leaving home semester by semester. I could hear a little teariness in Janet's voice whenever she talked. It would be hard for her to tell her son good-bye. In another couple of years, Kenny, now in high school, would be in college too. Maybe our developing friendship was as good for Janet as it was for me.

"We're going to San Antonio tomorrow, remember?" I told her. "There's a funeral service at the chapel first, then burial in the church cemetery nearby. It will give us a chance to pay respect to Professor Harrison, and maybe talk to his family. We might find out his reason for digging in our graveyard."

Janet cheered up a bit. "Will Martha McNair come with us?"

"I doubt it. Tomorrow's Monday. She's probably working at the library. I don't think she knows Professor Harrison anyway, except as a patron of the Yorktown public library."

"Oh."

"We'll know some people at the funeral. The professor's sister, Estelle Shawn, remember her? She's a lawyer; she gave us her card. And Gregory Jackson. He told me he plans to attend."

"He ought to get back to town. He's been around here a lot lately."

"Guess he's not welcome at his garage apartment. Estelle wanted to evict him, remember?"

Janet laughed. "We'll have to give him some support. I'd hate to have Estelle's opposition, wouldn't you? She seemed strong and, well, domineering. Probably always thinks she's right."

I hadn't given Estelle much thought, but Janet's assessment seemed exactly on the button.

"We'll see tomorrow," I told her. Jordan pulled the car into a nice shady parking space, and it was almost time for the service to begin. Time for us to scoot in.

We found the Judson family pew. Up ahead, behind the pulpit and the altar, there was space for the choir and the organ. Choir members wore dark blue robes. I could see Martha on the women's side of the choir, lined up with the altos and sopranos. I wondered if I would recognize any of the songs. I'd attended a church of a different denomination while growing up in Houston.

Music from the organ welcomed the pastor and the beginning of the service. It was a nice event, with a good sermon and a good choir. There were two solos, and Martha sang one of them. When the service ended, and everyone slowly walked down the central aisle toward the front door, I saw Bob Bennett, all dressed up in a pale gray suit with a maroon tie.

By the time I reached the front door along with Janet and the family, Bob was already there. The two of us said goodbye to the others and walked to Bob's car. We headed for Stockman's Restaurant and joined the crowd waiting to be seated. Martha and Allen were already there, signed up ahead of us. They were seated at a small round table in the bar area, where people waited to be called for their places in the restaurant.

Allen saw us and waved, inviting us over, so we joined them and ordered glasses of wine.

"We have an appointment this afternoon to look at the farmhouse for sale," Allen announced. "The one you told us about, Bob. Remember?"

"Sure I do. It's practically next door to me. Well, on the same road, anyway. Maybe we'll run into you again later on. I'm planning to introduce Caroline to my horses, my stock pond, my peach orchard, and maybe some of my cattle."

Under the table, he took my hand. I was surprised by his plan for the afternoon, but I liked it. I squeezed Bob's hand, and he squeezed mine back. Martha and Allen were called to their table, and Bob and I were left alone with our glasses of wine.

"You must have taken quite a liking to Allen and Martha," I said.

"I have. They seem very nice. I'd like to see a couple remodel that house down the road from me. I don't want it to stay empty forever, falling into disrepair. It needs some work, and not everyone could afford it."

I took a sip of wine and finally asked, "It doesn't matter to you that they are black?" I held my breath waiting for his answer.

"No," he said. "Why do you ask?"

I wasn't sure why his answer mattered to me, but it did. "Not many black people live in DeWitt County," I said. "I looked up the demographics when I moved here. It's different in a lot of ways from Houston."

"Houston." Bob made a face. "Yes, it's different. A different history from ours in some ways. I don't have any control over the past centuries of development here or in Houston, but as a constable I do everything I can to uphold civil rights. I spent some of my youth in a multicultural, multiracial environment, during my years in college and then in the Army. I spent a couple of years in Houston, working in an office where some of my colleagues were

Asian, Hispanic, or black. Then I got married and came back home with my wife, but it turned out she didn't like leaving Houston. Eventually she returned there and took our children with her."

The waiter brought us each another glass of wine. Bob lifted his. "I didn't want to move to Houston. I don't hold any grudges against people of other races or cultures, but I want to live where I grew up, here in DeWitt County."

"I remember visiting here as a child, but after Daddy passed away, we didn't come here much anymore. So I grew up in Houston. I like it here, though. I like being, um, enfolded by my family. I like feeling attached to my father's roots and learning about my branch of the family tree."

We shared a minute of silence, sipping our wine. "I must say I've encountered both racial attitudes here in DeWitt County, though," I said. "I think I already told you about the old man we met in our cemetery, who didn't want Professor Harrison buried there, and didn't care that he had been murdered. He's one of our relatives, and I'm ashamed to say so. But on the other side, there's Janet."

I finished my second glass of wine. "Janet is enchanted by Martha McNair and Allen Boyce, even by the rather bossy lady lawyer in San Antonio. She's intrigued by our plans for attending Professor Harrison's funeral and meeting his family. I think she's hardly ever made friends with any black people in her life here in Yorktown, and she enjoys having a chance to do so."

Bob laughed. "That's believable. Another thing, though, is that Janet is very warm-hearted. She likes everybody, and does what she can to provide help when needed. Hasn't she invited you to join the ladies' volunteer group at church?"

"She's mentioned it," I admitted. "I guess I'm one of her projects now. She does a lot to help me with my new life in Yorktown."

"You're more than a project," Bob said. "I can tell that. You're a cousin and a friend, and the friendship is steadily growing."

Bob's assessment made me smile. The waiter arrived and escorted us to our dinner table, and the topics of conversation changed. All the same, I cherished what he had said about Janet.

We looked at the menus and ordered our dinners, which arrived soon, and continued to chat about the differences between Houston and Yorktown. At the end of our meal, I asked Bob, "Do you mind stopping by my house when we leave? I'd like to change out of my Sunday clothes and wear something more casual."

"I'd like to change, too, if that's okay with you. I have some jeans and boots in my car."

We reached my house in about fifteen minutes and changed our clothes. Bob put his suit on a hangar and carefully placed it at the rear side window of his car. I made us a quick pot of coffee and, when Bob was back in the cottage, poured us each a cup. We sat on the sofa in the living room, enjoying my delicious mixture of regular coffee and hazelnut decaf.

Bob surveyed the living room, the adjacent kitchen, the study. "All the furnishings in this house came from Houston," I said. "They fit together pretty well here, although some things are too big for the small rooms of this cottage."

"Looks pretty to me. Very comfortable." He stood up and walked around, admiring the Oriental rugs on the hardwood floors, and the paintings hanging on the walls. "Is this your office?" he asked, looking at the study on one side of the living room.

We walked into the little room containing my desk, file cabinets, and trestle table loaded with stacks of books and papers. "All this has accumulated since moving here," I told Bob. "I haven't gone through all of it. It's more like research material. Whenever I want to find something out, this is the place to look."

Bob laughed. "I'll have to introduce you to my mother. You're a lot like her in some ways."

"Does she live with you at your country house—er, ranch house?"

"No, not any more. She lives with my brother and sister-in-law in Cuero. She needs more company and health care than I can provide, but Carla and Dennis can. It's working out very well. Mama used to live in my house, though. She and Daddy raised Dennis and me there. In fact, when Daddy died, I bought the house and land from her. Dennis didn't object, and I wanted to keep it in good shape. Keep it in the family. Dennis visits, but he likes living in Cuero."

"You're making me feel curious about seeing your place."

He gulped down the last of his coffee and set the cup down.. "I'm ready to go whenever you are."

"I'm ready, too." The cups went into the kitchen sink, and we went out toward the car. I grabbed my purse with pen and paper, just in case.

Soon we were chugging along on the red dirt roads. Bob drove slow to avoid raising too much dust. We were still in a drought; no rain, not many wildflowers. The roads began to look familiar, and soon we approached Uncle Cotton's place. I could see him out in the large area back of the house, standing in the pen with his pack of hound dogs.

"Why does my uncle keep so many dogs?" I asked Bob. "I'm sure you know the answer, and I haven't got a clue."

"He just likes them," Bob answered. "He uses them for hunting javelinas, and sells young, well-trained hounds to some extent, but mostly he likes them."

"Oh."

"He likes flowers, too." Bob gestured at the wide flower beds surrounding the brick ranch-style house. Beds of azaleas, roses, day lilies were already blooming, even though the wildflowers were not. Uncle Cotton must have taken good care of them with water and fertilizer.

"Have you heard about your uncle's wolf hunt coming up next week?"

I had to admit that I hadn't.

"I'm sure Janet will tell you about it. It's an occasional fun event for your uncle and his friends."

"They shouldn't be hunting wolves," I sniffed. "Wolves are practically extinct in this part of Texas."

"Maybe it really used to be a wolf hunt, just like the hunts in England were really fox hunts. But fox hunts in England have been outlawed, and the wolf hunts here feature a coyote, captured and released. The hunters don't ride horses, either. They use motorcycles, Jeeps, and pickup trucks. Instead of a hunting horn, they have CB radios that work in areas where cell phones don't."

"Good grief."

"They release the coyote, and then the hounds, then chase after them on motor vehicles and, if necessary, on foot. They may retrieve and release the coyote eventually, or it may get away on its own. However that turns out, the hunt ends back at Cotton's house where a barbecue is already underway."

"Barbecue of what?"

"Not a coyote!" Bob laughed. "Pork and beef barbecue with cornbread, beans, salad, and desserts. The wives bring home-made pies and cakes. There are bottles of beer and cups of coffee. If you want to hear old family stories told, this is a place to listen. Also, you might meet kinfolk who live some miles away but travel here for the wolf hunt. They'll usually stay up late and spend the night, then go home in the morning."

By this time, we had turned onto another road and left Uncle Cotton's place behind. "The wolf hunt sounds like fun," I said. "Will you be there?"

Bob looked crestfallen. "Probably not. I'm on duty during the day and on call that night. I might manage to get by for a while, but not for the whole thing."

"Too bad," I said. "I'll see if Janet and Jordan will take me. It's another new event for me, and I need Janet to give me an introduction. Hey, wait, where are we going?" Bob had turned the car off the road, onto a small, graveled lane.

"We're at my house," Bob said, and I could hear pride in his voice. The lane was bordered by barbed-wire fences left and right. Soon we reached a gate. Bob unlocked it, drove us through, and locked it behind us. Ahead of us stood a large white house whose big front porch was surrounded by beds of roses. To the right of the house was a water cistern and a big windmill; to the left, a vegetable garden. A porch swing, some tall-back rocking chairs and a small table decorated the porch, along with ceramic pots holding rosemary, parsley, sage, and other herbs.

"You must do some of your own cooking." I plucked a twig of rosemary and held it under my nose, enjoying the strong fragrance.

"Some, but not much. I like growing the herbs and vegetables, but I bring baskets of tomatoes and okra into the office. I share it with my colleagues."

He opened the front door. "Let's go in and I'll make a pot of coffee." I could tell by his voice that he was teasing me; he must have noticed how much coffee I brewed at home to drink. I took him up on the offer. "Sounds like a good idea to me."

We walked through the big front room of his house and into the country-style kitchen, where he went to the sink area and ran water for the pot of coffee. I took a seat at the large wooden table with a dozen chairs.

An antique pie safe decorated one wall of the kitchen. The wooden cabinet's doors had metal panels with designs pierced into them to let air in and out. Its legs ended in metal wheels that sat in bowls of water to keep ants from crawling up to the shelves holding pies. I'd seen pie safes in country museums and antique stores, but not in anyone's house.

I noticed that this pie safe's water bowls were dry, and figured that Bob used contemporary pest control to keep ants out.

Bob came to the table with a tray holding cups of coffee, sugar, cream, napkins, and spoons. I stirred sugar and cream into my coffee, and took a sip of it. "Delicious," I told Bob. "You must do this on a regular basis."

To my surprise, he blushed. "I eat meals out most of the time, but I usually fix my own breakfast. Coffee's the start of the day. It gets me up and going."

"Oh, I know what you mean. It keeps me going, too." I looked around the kitchen and the adjacent big front room. "This house must have been built some time ago for a big family."

"My great-grandparents built it in 1910, a hundred years ago. Some of their children lived here with them, including my grandfather and his wife and kids. My father inherited the house and land eventually. When he died, and I bought the house from my mother, I was still married and my family lived here with me. There was plenty of room for my wife and two sons. We modernized the house to some extent. See the kitchen cabinets and the new sink, and the dishwasher? When I was growing up here, it was different. The original kitchen was still in place."

I remembered Grandma Gussie's old-fashioned kitchen in her much smaller house. It had been updated, and one of Maury's young sons lived there now. "Your kitchen looks beautiful," I told Bob. "The hardwood floors, the pie safe, the huge old table blend well with the new kitchen cabinets."

I looked through the large doorway into the front room. Two quilts hanging on the walls had caught my attention, one on each side of the front doorway.

"Grandma Gussie used to quilt," I said. "Who made your quilts? They look great."

"My grandmother made those." Bob stirred a little more cream into his coffee. "Both won prizes at a county fair. She made dozens more. Some are in the bedrooms upstairs, some are in Dennis's house in Cuero, some have been used up and fallen to pieces."

"Sounds familiar. Our families have that in common." I smiled at Bob and he smiled back at me.

He reached out for my empty coffee cup. "Ready to take a look at my horses and cows?" He finished his own coffee and put the cups in the sink.

Soon we were out the door and back in the car, driving down

the lane toward the barn with the horses' stables. Right now, though, the stables were empty and the horses were out in a pasture. Two little colts were with their mothers, and with the third mare, another was on the way. We stopped the car and admired the horses then Bob pointed at the group of cattle clustered at the far end of another pasture.

"I usually drive my truck out here. The lane peters out and I don't want to drive the car over there. Let's turn around and go check out the stock pond."

The lane was broad and well-traveled all the way to the large stock pond. Because of the drought, its level was low, but the pier still jutted out over the water, and a rowboat rested under the pier on the dry shore.

Bob pulled the car to a parking space under an oak tree. You could see the lane leading to the pier and rowboat, the stock pond with ducks and geese on its reedy edges. A few wildflowers were in bloom around it.

Bob and I sat in silence, watching the sun glint off the pond's water, enjoying the oak's cool shade. After a while, I turned my head to look at Bob, but he was already looking at me.

"Carrie," he whispered, and took my face between his hands. I didn't resist; I leaned toward him, and he kissed me, slowly and sweetly. Then his strong arms swept me toward him, and the kisses were ardent and long.

At last we pulled away from each other, gasping, hearts pounding. Bob's hands were trembling.

"We'd better stop," he said, and I reluctantly agreed. He leaned back in the car seat and waited for his body to relax.

"You're going to Harrison's funeral tomorrow, right?" he asked at last.

"Yes. Janet's driving."

"Can I take you to dinner tomorrow night?"

"Seven o'clock?"

"That's fine. I'll be off work by then."

He leaned over and kissed me again, then said, "I'll pick you up at your house at seven." He started the car and soon we were on the dirt roads, driving me home.

CHAPTER TEN
Monday, March 22, 2010

The funeral home in East Side San Antonio serenely faced Commerce Street. A large new building made of brick, it was graced by large Corinthian pillars, a circular driveway, and a small front lawn planted with orderly, well-trimmed trees and shrubs. A large paved lot in the back accommodated parking. Sidewalks led around the building to the double front door. It opened into a lobby where Professor Thomas Harrison's sister stood, along with a few other family members. Entering the lobby, Janet and I saw Estelle and headed toward her.

"Do you remember us, Estelle?" I asked, speaking quietly. "We met at your brother's house a few days ago. We were visiting San Antonio and stopped by, hoping there would be someone to talk to. We belong to the Hargrove family, you see. It's our family cemetery where Professor Harrison was found. We deeply regret his death, and came here today to pay our respects."

Estelle's expression changed while I was speaking. At first, she glared at us with anger, then realized we weren't gambling debt collectors after all, and calmed down. "I'd like to talk to you, but I don't have extra time now. Are you going to our cemetery for the burial?"

We nodded. "We'd like to talk to you if you have time later on."

"We will. We'll work it out. There's a reception after the burial. Just look for me before you leave the cemetery, and I'll direct you." She shook our hands then turned to the couple approaching her, greeting them. "Marvin, Linda, how good of you to come."

Janet and I walked on, leaving the lobby and entering a large room with pews for seating. A coffin sat at the front of the room, surrounded by a huge bank of floral arrangements. The coffin was open, and a line of people filed by slowly, stopping to take a last look at Thomas Harrison and tell him farewell.

Janet nudged me. "Do you want to go tell him goodbye?"

I thought about it. "Not really. I remember seeing him at our cemetery when we found him. That's enough. Let's just find a seat."

We selected a place on the side of the room. The crowd was growing larger and a family section of several pews up front, marked off with mourning ribbons, was filling up. The family consisted of some people looking older than the professor and his sister Estelle. Parents, aunts and uncles, I guessed. Others looked about the age of Estelle and the professor. Sisters, brothers, cousins, and their spouses. There were younger ones, too. Teen-agers and grade-schoolers, all taking off one more spring break day. Tomorrow they'd go back to school.

In particular, I noticed a young black man, standing with the family but not talking to anyone. He wore a navy blue suit with a striped tie; he had a closely cropped haircut and a mustache; and he wore gold-wire-rimmed glasses. I wondered if he was a member of the family or a student or friend of the professor. He looked in my direction and I was afraid he'd think I was staring at him, so I looked away from him

Looking around the whole room, I noticed that Janet and I weren't the only Caucasians present. The crowd must have included the professor's colleagues, friends, and students from the university; neighbors from Dignowity Hill; friends and acquaintances from social clubs and activities. White, black, Hispanic, and Asian friends and family had come to pray for Thomas Harrison's soul, his eternal life, his entrance into heaven. They had come to tell him they would see him later.

Across the room there was a young man who looked like Gregory Jackson, but he was so far away I couldn't be sure.

Cemetery Whites

Half an hour passed as the funeral home filled up. At eleven o'clock, the funeral service began. A pastor conducted it as a religious service, including prayers, hymns, a brief sermon, and a eulogy.

At last it was over. Six pallbearers approached the coffin. The funeral home director stepped forward and slid the coffin's cover into place. Thomas Harrison was closed off to the world and ready for burial. The pallbearers took their places, three on each side. They lifted the coffin from its stand and walked slowly down the central aisle toward the lobby and the front door.

The pastor left the pulpit, the organist played some music, and the ushers began directing departure of the crowd, pew by pew. The family members left their pews first, and slowly followed the pallbearers. The ushers then directed departure of people from a pew on one side of the room and then the other. Janet and I, seated close to the front of the room, were soon following the family and the pallbearers with the coffin.

The front doors of the building were wide open, and a hearse stood in the circular driveway. The pallbearers carried the coffin toward it, the driver opened its back doors, and the pallbearers slid the coffin into it.

The church cemetery was two blocks away. Some people headed for the parking lot and drove their cars to the cemetery, parking on the street nearby. Others departed, not staying for the burial. Janet and I joined the majority, walking down the shaded sidewalk toward the cemetery with the family plot.

By the time we arrived, the hearse had delivered the coffin, which was suspended over the open grave. The family stood at the foot of it, and others stood nearby. The pastor appeared, and, when everyone had assembled, led us through the burial rite.

The coffin was lowered into the grave, and a shovel full of dirt flung onto it. Family members came forward and each dropped a red rose onto the coffin. Sobs broke out, and the pastor concluded the ceremony. People said their prayers, said goodbye, then turned

Connie Knight

and walked away. Some were going back to work, and some would attend the reception Estelle had told Janet and me about.

"It's at my mother's house," she'd said, hurriedly talking to us on the way from the funeral parlor to the cemetery. "I live there with her, by the way." She'd thrust a hand-drawn map into my hand then sped forward to walk with her family.

Janet and I turned from the grave and walked back to the maroon sedan. Opened Estelle's map and looked at it.

"This is in the same area as the professor's house," I told Janet. "Do you remember how to get there?"

"I can get us to New Braunfels Avenue and the big historic cemetery—the one we visited. Can you direct me from there?"

"Sure. That will work."

Cars leaving the parking lot were also heading for New Braunfels Avenue. We got into Janet's car and joined the line waiting to exit, then followed them toward the avenue. The traffic became heavy, and the cars scattered, but as we followed Estelle's directions, they began to regroup near Dignowity Park. The cars were parked up and down Randolph Street, and the drivers walked toward the same house. I slid Estelle's map into my purse. We followed the crowd.

One member of the crowd was the young man I'd noticed at the funeral home. I was walking right behind him on the crowded sidewalk when I stumbled on a cracked square of cement. Oak tree roots had raised part of it higher than the rest.

I fell forward and bumped heavily into the young man before I managed to straighten myself up. Before I could open my mouth to apologize, he had whirled around, scowled at me, and made a blistering remark of his own.

"When you're throwing your weight around, be ready to get thrown around by somebody else," he said. His voice was surly and his fists were clenched.

As it happened, I recognized his saying, one of many from the old Texas days, one I'd heard before. "Well, who stuck the burr under your saddle?" I said, responding with the first old saying that came to my mind.

He didn't think that was funny. Fortunately, a gray-haired lady, perhaps his mother, stepped in.

"Josh Gaines, you unclench your fists right now," she said to him. "Don't you even think this lady bumped into you deliberately. You should apologize for your reaction. It was only an accident."

"I apologize," I said quickly. "I tripped on the sidewalk, and I'm sorry I bumped into you. It wasn't on purpose."

Josh gave the gray-haired lady a sideways glance. He loosened his fists, and he seemed calm. "I apologize, too," he said. "I'm sorry for the way I reacted. Your bump took me by surprise. I'm sorry."

I extended my hand and he grasped it in his. We shook hands and smiled. "Maybe we can chat later and get acquainted," I said. He nodded, and we resumed our walk toward the reception.

The house was a large, two-story Victorian, nicely restored, with azalea bushes in bloom around the front porch. We entered the foyer, recognized people from the funeral services, and looked for Estelle Shawn. She saw us before we saw her, and walked over to greet us.

Her eyes were somber, and I could tell she had been crying. Janet found a pack of tissues in her purse, and handed it to Estelle. "What's the matter?" she said with concern. "We can see you another time if you prefer."

Estelle used the tissues to wipe her eyes. "No, let's talk now." She motioned us to follow her. From the foyer, we went through a heavy sliding door into a large room on one side of the house. It was a library with cushioned, comfortable sofas and chairs. Dark wood panels covered the walls. The built-in book shelves were also made of dark wood. Estelle switched on a lamp or two, and waved at a table near the room's windows. She pulled out a chair for herself. "Please join me," she said, and we did.

Sitting at the small table, we were all quiet for a few moments. Estelle took a deep breath. "You said you are members of the

Hargrove family? Something about the cemetery where my brother's body was found?"

"This is my cousin Janet Hargrove Judson, and I'm Caroline Hargrove Hamilton. Our family cemetery is in DeWitt County. Janet and I went there one morning recently and we found your brother. His body. We called the constable who responded quickly."

"Constable Bennett?"

"Yes. You've been talking to him, haven't you? He must have told you about the ongoing investigation, but so far not much has materialized. Our family is concerned about—um, the murder—the death of your brother. Our cemetery is way out in the country, and we don't want it to be a place where bad things can happen. We had a family meeting, and I volunteered to serve as an amateur detective. To see what I could find out. Janet's been working on the project with me. I'll be glad to tell you what we've discovered, and I hope you can tell us why Professor Harrison was digging in our cemetery in the first place."

"Please tell me first. Tell me how you found my brother."

I gave Estelle a full account of the morning Janet drove me to the Hargrove Family Cemetery and how we found her brother's body. How we called the constable and were present for the officers' arrival and investigation, how we saw the ambulance technicians zip the professor into a body bag and put him into the ambulance, then drive off.

"There are a few more personal things," I told Estelle, and related the significance of the site of her brother's death. "He was digging for something at the foot of my great-great-great-grandfather's grave, where there's a big patch of white irises that were in bloom. We found him lying in the irises, still clutching his shovel."

"What happened with the relatives you said drove him there? Your aunt and her son?"

"Grandson," I corrected. "Great-Aunt Hettie and Donny." I told Estelle about Hettie's gunshot, and how we had found her

Cemetery Whites

bullet in the branch of an oak tree. "There was a second shot at the same time Aunt Hettie's gun went off. We're trying to find out who it was, but so far we haven't found any real suspects, and neither has Constable Bennett, to our knowledge."

Estelle sighed. "Thank you for telling me. I've heard some of it from Constable Bennett, but your own personal experiences add a lot to his official account. I appreciate it. Tom's interest in your cemetery must have had something to do with Texas history. That was the core of his career."

"Something about the Sutton-Taylor Feud? Apparently that was related to the second corpse in my great-great-great-grandfather's grave."

Estelle shrugged. "Maybe. I really don't know. The teaching assistant might be able to help you. Gregory Jackson, who lives in the garage apartment. He and Tom were working together on something for quite a while."

"We've talked to him already, but I guess we could do that again."

Estelle walked over to a nearby desk and opened a shallow drawer. She pulled out a couple of small booklets. "Will these help? Tom had them made. It's a family history. He had them printed for a family reunion about five years ago."

Estelle handed me a booklet and gave one to Janet. I opened mine and looked at it with interest. There were photographs of houses, stores, family members, and diagrams of the family tree. At the head of the tree, but off to the side, were Willie Gaines and his mother Priscilla, dressed nicely and obviously living in San Antonio when the picture was taken.

"What in the world?" I stammered. What did Priscilla and Willie, associated with John David Hargrove's wife Sarah Gaines, have to do with the Harrisons?

Estelle looked at the page I pointed at. "That's as far back as we can get," she said. "Tom did the research, so I don't really know more than is here in print."

I quit stammering and started sputtering. "I know more than Tom put in writing. Willie and Priscilla were slaves who came to Texas with my great-great-grandparents John David Hargrove and Sarah Gaines. So did Priscilla's husband, Josiah. He died on the way, but Priscilla and Willie stayed with Sarah Gaines Hargrove until well after the Civil War. I just found this out a few days ago, when I was looking through papers my cousin Miranda gave me. "

Estelle looked astonished. I continued, "When Janet and I visited the historic cemetery on New Braunfels Avenue a few days age, we found Priscilla Gaines. Her grave, I mean. It's in the black section of the old cemetery. John David and Sarah Hargrove are buried there, too, but in a different section. They moved from DeWitt County to San Antonio and built a house just a few blocks from where we are right now."

"Well, why didn't Tom include this information, if it's true?" Estelle demanded. She didn't know whether to believe me, or her brother's gaps in his booklet's history.

"I don't know. I don't think it's that hard to find in genealogy research."

"Maybe he didn't think it was so important," Estelle said, studying the booklet. "The real founder of this family, although he was named Josiah Gaines, was an orphan. Priscilla and her son Willie raised him here in San Antonio. He became a successful businessman and the father of quite a few children, who became successful too. Our Harrison family is a branch from the Gaineses. That was my mother's last name."

We looked at each other, pondering. What could we do next? Did the past have anything to do with Thomas Harrison's death?

Janet broke the silence. "Estelle, there are a lot of documents in my family that might have something to do with yours. Caroline mentioned researching the history of Priscilla and Willie, and I'll help however I can. Would you like copies of whatever we find?"

"Yes." Estelle's voice became rough with emotion. "We may find something Tom was looking for. It could be in your papers, or it could be in mine."

"Yours? What do you mean?"

"There's a box of old papers up in the attic here. Tom never knew about them, and I never told him. He could be so arrogant! He thought he already knew everything, and I was just his little sister—anyway, I never told him about the box in the attic. Besides, in the past few years, when he started going to rooster fights and gambling on them, he stopped visiting us very often."

Estelle walked over to a large, heavy closet door made of burnished dark wood. She opened it and switched on a light. A staircase led up to the next floor, turned, and continued up to the attic. Estelle flipped light switches as we followed her. When we reached it, the attic was well-lighted. It held boxes, trunks, old furniture. Estelle walked over to an old cedar chest, opened it, rummaged around, and found a sturdy white cardboard box.

"Grandma Gaines gave this to me years ago. I made sure it didn't get lost or destroyed, but I never read all these papers."

She tucked the box under her arm and the three of us retraced our steps. When we reached the library, Estelle closed the door to the staircase, and the three of us stared at the box she placed on the table.

"Let's make copies," Estelle finally said. "There's a copy machine in my office. It'll take a while. Can you wait?"

We agreed. Estelle led us to a small room adjacent to the library. It was her home office, furnished with desk, computer, file cabinets, and a copy machine. She placed the papers carefully on the glass top of the machine, one at a time. The papers were original and couldn't be fed through; they might have been torn or destroyed. I gathered the copies as they slid out, and stacked them into appropriate piles of letters, journals, invoices, whatever.

When we finished, Estelle searched her desk for a large envelope and packed the papers into it. She handed it to me.

"I hope this helps you with your research on your family and mine, especially whatever it was that Tom was up to."

"Thank you, Estelle. Let's keep in touch. Is your e-mail address on the business card you gave me?"

Someone knocked on the library door. "Estelle? Are you in there? Mama's looking for you."

"I'll be along in a minute," Estelle called back. She told me, "The e-mail's on the card," and darted toward the door. "Let's get together next time you're in town."

She slipped out the door with the white box under her arm, leaving Janet and me behind. We waited a few minutes, then slipped out the door too, and walked on to what was left of the reception.

Not many people were left, none that we knew except Estelle. She was busy with other people, so Janet and I decided to leave.

On the way out, we stopped in the foyer and signed our names in the guest book. We had paid our respects to Thomas Harrison at his funeral and burial, and our names showed our dutiful attendance.

CHAPTER ELEVEN

Evening of Monday, March 22, 2010

It was almost four o'clock when Janet and I drove up to my cottage in Yorktown. We'd had a quiet drive from San Antonio, each of us mulling over the events of the day. I'd clutched the envelope Estelle had given me, but didn't open it up yet. I wanted plenty of time to spread things out and look them over.

"I have to see the dentist again tomorrow morning," Janet reminded me. "Want to get together after lunch?"

I collected my purse and pen and paper, along with the envelope. "Sure. How about two o'clock? Maybe I'll have some news from organizing these documents."

"We could go to the library, too, and see if Martha can find any more information for us. Besides, I'd like to hear if she and Allen liked the old farmhouse they looked at."

"We'll do that." I stepped out of the car with my hands full, managed to close the car door and wave goodbye. I opened the door to my house and headed for the study, where I set the envelope in the center of the trestle table.

A sudden wave of exhaustion swept over me, and I decided to take a break. I changed my funeral dress for a pair of comfortable jeans and a cotton tee shirt. An English muffin and a cup of coffee revived my level of energy, and I was back in the study before an hour passed. I glanced at the clock. Bob would pick me up for dinner at seven, but I had some time to look at the documents.

I sat down at the trestle table, picked up the envelope, opened it, and slid out the stack of papers. I decided to organize them, and sorted them into piles of letters from Priscilla to Willie, Willie to Priscilla, and letters to both of them from Sarah Gaines Hargrove.

That was surprising. Then I realized the letters were from the time when Priscilla had accompanied Caroline Jane to New Mexico. Her son Willie was still in Texas, but by that time he had moved to San Antonio. Sarah and John David still lived on the ranch

There weren't any letters from Caroline Jane. She must have written some to her mother, but they weren't included in the Gaines family's package. Maybe there were some in the stacks of letters I'd already received from Miranda. I took a red pen and went through the Gaines package, marking each page with a red G in the upper right corner, and sorted them by date. Most of them had dates, thank goodness. The undated ones I set aside.

Methodically, I took Miranda's package and organized its letters by dates as well. It was a bigger package, with letters from early colonization and the Civil War years. All the same, I proceeded with organizing all documents by date. I was making progress. Then the doorbell rang.

I jumped, and looked at my wristwatch. It was seven o'clock, and that must be Bob Bennett at the door.

I looked through the peephole before opening the door. It was Bob, and he looked hungry. "Come on in," I told him. "I've been going through papers and lost track of time. Do you want to go to Stockman's? Or I could fix something here instead, and I'll show you the papers if you want to see them. Estelle Shawn gave them to me after the funeral today."

Bob gave a quick answer. "Sure. Dinner and papers—sounds good."

"Well, come into the kitchen and let's put something together."

The coffee pot was still full, so I poured us each a cup of coffee then put a quick dinner together, starting with an appetizer plate of crackers and cheese. There were plenty of leftovers in the fridge. Dinner consisted of green salad, chicken breast, herbed rice and fresh green beans. I served us at my little kitchen table and told Bob

Cemetery Whites

all about the day in San Antonio—the funeral service, the burial, the reception afterwards, and the revelation of the Harrisons branching from the orphan who was raised by Priscilla Gaines and her son Willie, both of whom had been associated with the Hargrove family before and after the Civil War.

"The families lost touch somehow. Willie moved to San Antonio at some point, and Priscilla joined him later on. She accompanied Caroline Jane out West, but didn't stay there. Estelle didn't know about the Hargroves, and I knew about the Gaineses but not that they were grandparents of the Harrisons. The connection became apparent when Estelle gave me a family history booklet with Priscilla and Willie included. The orphan they raised was named Josiah Gaines, after Priscilla's husband who died young, and he, the orphan, was the founder of the San Antonio Gaines family."

"Aha. I see." Bob didn't look like he really understood the family histories in detail. "You sound like my mother," he said at last. "She's followed our family history for years, and can still tell you everything about everybody."

I laughed. "I wish I knew everything. I just know a little, and I'm trying to learn a lot."

We'd finished dinner, so I removed the plates and poured us each a fresh cup of coffee. I brought in the stack of papers from Miranda and Estelle, collated by date, and the smaller stack with no date, waiting for the right place to be found.

"These papers interest me for family history altogether, but the history between Harrisons, Gaineses, and Hargroves is intriguing. It must have had something to do with Professor Harrison's presence in our cemetery, don't you think?"

Bob nodded. "I don't understand what he was digging for, though."

"I don't, either."

"But it might have provided a motive for someone to shoot Harrison. Maybe somebody didn't want him to turn up whatever he was looking for."

"It could have been old Uncle Henry, or somebody else like him. Racist."

"Or somebody who knew something we still don't. Something about the gambling debt, maybe."

"Oh well. Maybe something new will turn up eventually." I gathered the stack of papers. Bob didn't seem really interested in reading them. I noticed it was almost nine o'clock.

"Want to save the papers for later and watch something now on TV?"

Bob liked the idea. He grinned. We went into the living room, settled down on the sofa, and found a show to watch. Then Bob's arm went around me and pulled me close. I found myself leaning against him, my head on his shoulder. We watched the TV show, but it wasn't the most important thing on our minds.

Bob left at ten o'clock, when the show ended. We agreed to get together again on Wednesday.

"That's day after tomorrow. I have to work late on Tuesday and Thursday, especially Thursday. That's your uncle's wolf hunt night, remember?"

"Guess I'll miss you that night. I'm not planning to attend."

"Wednesday, then. I'll pick you up at seven."

We walked to the front door. He leaned down and kissed me goodbye. "Thanks for dinner," he said, and the door closed behind him.

I went back to the sofa and sat there by myself watching the ten o'clock news. It wasn't the most important thing on my mind. I was thinking about my husband Craig Hamilton, who died in a clumsy, futile car accident. Not a whit of it was his fault. He stayed late at work and drove home on a rainy night. The freeways were crowded, and for some reason a drunk driver, speeding, slammed on his brakes, causing his car to skid into Craig's, which rammed into another one. Six cars were involved in the accident. Drivers and passengers were seriously injured, but Craig was the only one who died.

Numbness, anger, searing grief had possessed me in Houston for well over a year. If I fell out of touch with former friends, maybe it was partly my choice. They tried to comfort me, but I wasn't ready to be comforted. By the time I could accept my loss, I wanted to leave Houston. My Yorktown family offered me a form of comfort I thought I could accept.

My trial of living in Yorktown was working out. Janet's friendship really helped, with her willingness to drive me around and introduce me to other people and activities. Her husband Jordan, cousin Maury and his wife Elizabeth, cousins Donny and Danny, their father Darryl and their grandmother, my Great-Aunt Hettie, all accepted and welcomed me, not to mention the larger crowd I'd met at the family meeting.

Then there was Bob. Not family, but a friend. By now, I have said goodbye to Craig. I still love him, but I know he's gone. There's room in my heart for friendship and a little romance, perhaps growing, with Bob.

Eleven o'clock. I was not sleepy yet. My newspaper column was due tomorrow, and I hadn't worked on it yet. Maybe I had some time.

The historic papers went back to the trestle table, and I brought my pens and pad of paper to the kitchen table. I began to write.

Going to the Country...

My name is Caroline Hargrove Hamilton, and I've just moved to Yorktown, to live with my Daddy's family who settled here in the days of the DeWitt Colony. When I was a child, more than 40 years ago, my father would drive his wife and children from San Antonio to his mother's house in the country. I remember those trips, but after Daddy died from injuries sustained in Viet Nam, Mama moved us to Houston and we seldom drove to visit Daddy's family. But I remember those trips with Daddy—one in particular.

Connie Knight

It was a long drive from San Antonio to Oak Creek, Texas, where Grandma Gussie and my cousin Maury lived. Once we reached DeWitt County, the drive was better. The woods started—scrubby oaks, interspersed with grass fields dotted with cactus. We turned onto a caliche dirt road. It was bright red, so there must have been a rain. We children watched for landmarks. "There's the bridge! There's the cistern! There's Grandma's windmill!"

Daddy pulled up the car at Grandma's gate with a screech, and the dogs in the yard started barking. The guinea hens set up a racket; out back, a rooster crowed, just to get in on the act. Cousin Maury came whooping out the door, followed more slowly by Grandma, hollering, "Maur-eee! Come back and close that door."

The sky was bleak and steely-gray, and a cold wind was blowing. I followed everyone into the house, crossing the little wood-floored porch whose planks were dark and soggy with rain. Inside, in the large front room, wood was burning in the black iron stove. The wood-box nearby was full of logs; they smelled sharp and funny. What was that square thing hanging from the ceiling? Was that a quilt stretched on it? Grandma Gussie made so many quilts. Tonight, a stack of them would be spread on the front room floor, making pallets where my sisters and I and our cousins would sleep.

I went to the kitchen to get a drink of water. Grandma came in, speaking to me in her slow voice that had a grating texture like the mineral crust around the faucet. Maybe that's what happens if you drink hard water. What did Grandma say? "Yes, Ma'am," I answered, pretending to have heard.

"Well, take one then," said Grandma, and I understood she had offered me a cookie. I took one from the still-warm baking pan. Was there molasses in it? Grandma believed in Black Draught syrup and black-strap molasses. She dipped snuff, too. It came in a brown glass jar, square in shape and stopped with a piece of cork. The three bottles all stood together on a shelf above the stove. Maybe Grandma got them mixed up? I nibbled my cookie anyway, and wandered out to the front room where the other children were

112

Cemetery Whites

already playing Fish.

Whenever we visited Maury, we played Fish.

Whenever we played Fish, Maury won.

What would it be like to be Maury, and live with Grandma always? He had to chop wood in the morning, and build the fire in the stove. On the other hand, he hunted for eggs in the chicken coop every single day.

Mama came in and saw me sitting by myself. "Don't you want to play cards with the other children?" she said, wheedling. She hated to see me all alone.

I whined, "Mama, I want to go home."

Mama leaned forward and scolded me. "Don't embarrass me in front of your Grandma Gussie!"

The game of Fish stopped, and I saw by my sisters' faces that they felt sorry for me, but thought I had it coming. "I didn't want to come here," I shouted at all of them. "I wanted to stay home!"

"I'm at my wit's end with you!" said Mama. "Just be quiet now!"

Her scolding upset me, and I turned away, sobbing quietly. "I'm adopted," I whispered. Once said, the words assumed authority, as if a truth had been revealed. I drifted into the kitchen and got myself a cookie, mulling over the new point of view the word contained. "I'm adopted. Someday I'll run away and find my real parents."

I sat down at the kitchen table, not noticing the presence of my cousin Lillian. But Lillian saw me and heard me talking about adoption.

"I used to think that too," she said. "But I've changed my mind. I know I come from here, and so do you."

I sniffled and asked her, "How do you know?"

"There's Grandma's Bible. It's got a list of the family in it. I'm there and so are you. Then there are the pictures that were taken."

Lillian looked through the kitchen door into Grandma's bedroom. Framed photographs stood in multitude on her dresser.

Connie Knight

"Take a look at those and you'll find someone who looks like you."

"I don't know if I want to look like any of them," I said.

"Like it or not, you do," Lillian said. "They're wearing old-fashioned clothes. That's what makes the difference."

"Who will I be like then?"

"That's up to you," Lillian said. "Just think about it before you make up your mind." She stood up and walked away.

I stayed at the table, and was quiet. I wasn't adopted after all.

All the same, it took me years to find my way home from Houston to DeWitt County. I've been here less than a month, and I'm just settling in. My cousin Janet is showing me around, and I'm researching family history, with special help from my cousin Miranda. I've found a church to attend, a library, two restaurants, and a barbecue place with a pool room and a wonderful band. I'm becoming reacquainted with my family, and I'm making some friends.

I owe belated thanks to my cousin Lillian, wherever she is. She helped me find my identity. Who could ask for more?

Cemetery Whites

CHAPTER TWELVE
Tuesday, March 23, 2010

I woke up early on Tuesday morning. I'd set the alarm for seven, and by eight o'clock I arrived at the Yorktown *Chronicle* with my column in my hand. Barry Wilson, the editor, took the papers from me. "Have a seat. I want to look this over."

He waved me to a chair near his desk. I sat down and held my breath while he read my column.

It didn't take long. "That'll do fine," he said, fastening the pages together with a paper clip. "I'll have Brenda typeset this. Next week, can you e-mail me your column by Monday? That will give us time to discuss it, and we can use the copy from the e-mail, of course, instead of retyping it."

Brenda took my photograph to put in the newspaper, and Mr. Morton in the accounting department cut me a check for fifty dollars.

I arrived at Casa Rosa happy and hungry and was soon tucking into my *huevos a la Mexicana* and a fresh cup of coffee. A copy of last week's Yorktown *Chronicle* still sat on a table near the cash register, and I picked it up to review the Sutton-Taylor Feud story again.

The story was familiar; I'd read it more than once before. I studied the photograph, which had been taken in the cemetery only a couple of hours after the professor's body had been removed. Danny was standing by Thomas Watson Hargrove's grave and carrying a rifle. In the photograph, the rifle was not pictured in detail, but the caption called it "a vintage Henry .44 rifle dating from the 1850s".

If Danny had access to the antique rifle, it must be in the current possession of his grandmother. My Great-Aunt Hettie.

I wondered who had owned the rifle originally. How had it passed down from one generation to the next? Did it still work? Could it still be used?

Of course, it wasn't the gun that killed Professor Harrison. That had been identified as a Glock handgun. About the rifle, I was just curious.

Aunt Hettie would have the answers, I thought. Maybe Janet and I could visit her in the afternoon. Meantime, I'd go home and take a look at those stacks of collated papers.

Once at home, I tackled the project. I knew I couldn't get through the entire stack of papers, so I set aside the older ones from colonization and Civil War, and focused on the Gaines letters collated with others from the same days. That started in 1875, when Caroline Jane took off for the West.

Of course, the letters didn't contain what might have been discussed in person when the letter writers could meet face-to-face. Journals documented private thoughts, but there weren't any in my stack of documents. There were some summaries written by cousin Miranda, and copies of oral histories collected in 1986, the Texas Sesquicentennial. Oral histories were printed in a separate book for each of our 254 counties, and something from the Hargroves appeared in more book than one.

I gathered my pens and paper pad, and settled down to read the letters and make notes.

I started by re-reading cousin Miranda's account of Caroline Jane. She and Priscilla's son Willie had worked together as children, especially during the Civil War when the men were gone. They managed the farm, did some hunting, and fought the Indians who resumed raiding during the Civil War, when men of the households were absent. After the Civil War, when Caroline Jane married James Jamison, Willie moved to the remote ranch with them. Eventually, with Jamison so involved with the Sutton-Taylor Feud, Caroline Jane managed the ranch and Willie became her foreman.

Didn't guns play into this, with the hunting, fighting raids, and protecting the lonely, isolated ranch? Miranda wrote that James Jamison became "physically abusive". Eventually Caroline Jane left the ranch and fled to the Hargrove homestead. Jamison followed her, and the family had agreed at our meeting that Jamison was the one who had been shot and then buried first in the grave dug for Thomas Watson Hargrove. The family secret had finally been acknowledged, though who did the shooting was still a mystery. Caroline Jane joined her brother Tom in traveling to Arizona; Priscilla accompanied her; Willie eventually ended up in San Antonio.

I began by reading the letters Priscilla wrote to Sarah, and others she wrote to her son Willie. They were brief and read like a travelogue, describing the landscape, the neighbors riding in other wagons, the food, the cattle and horses being driven along with the wagon train.

I had thought they might travel to Arizona by railroad train, but in 1875 the route going West from San Antonio was still under construction. Instead, they joined a wagon train, buying a wagon and equipment of their own, and bringing Tom's ranch animals with them.

In several months, they crossed the plains, hit the Pecos River, and followed it upstream into New Mexico. From there, they headed for Tucson, Arizona.

In Priscilla's letters, I noticed her references to Caroline Jane's use of her rifle in hunting and Indian fights. Priscilla wrote about them in an off-hand way, as if they should be taken for granted, but at least in the TV Western shows I'd seen while growing up, women on a wagon train would tend to cooking and taking care of the children. What was up with Caroline Jane and her rifle? She sounded like another Annie Oakley.

Sarah's letters written to Priscilla, and to Willie as well, expressed her concern for their well-being, and questions about the welfare of her children Tom and Caroline Jane. She seemed to think she would never see any of them again. She mentioned receiving letters from Caroline Jane, so there were some even though they didn't appear in the Hargrove or Gaines collections.

Willie wrote to his mother and to Sarah, whom he addressed as Mrs. Sarah Hargrove. At first in San Antonio he stayed with a family, former slaves from DeWitt County, who had moved to the city and were living in Ellis Alley, an integrated area. Willie found a job at a local church, where I knew from the Gaines family booklet he had stayed for years.

By the time the wagon train reached Tucson, Caroline Jane had fallen ill, and winter was approaching. Tom took the cattle and horses to his new ranch, where Caroline and Priscilla could join him in the spring. Meantime, they would stay in Tucson, with lodgings arranged for the winter.

By the time I covered this much history in so many letters, it was one o'clock and I was hungry as a bear that Caroline Jane might shoot. I set the letters, and my notes, aside on the trestle table and went into the kitchen.

I made myself a ham sandwich on whole wheat toast. I ate my lunch at the kitchen table, mulling over all the letters I had read so far.

Where were the letters from Caroline Jane, and those written to her? They must have been culled out. Had they been saved in a separate box, or burned up for some reason?

I nibbled on a cookie with my cup of coffee, and pondered over the letters.

Finally I decided to ask Aunt Hettie about Caroline Jane when I asked her about the Henry rifle. Maybe it was Caroline's rifle, retrieved from the West, but what would that have to do with anything?

My cell phone rang. It was two o'clock, and Janet and her maroon sedan were waiting outside for me. I gathered up my purse,

Cemetery Whites

pens, and pad of paper. The stack of letters on the trestle table would have to wait for my return before I continued reading them.

I locked the front door behind me and joined Janet, who had just finished at the dentist's office. Her jaw was swollen and she lisped whenever she tried to talk.

"I'm tho hungry I could eat a cow, but I'm not thuppothed to eat anything until my numb feeling goeth away. Maybe we can have thome dinner after while? Jordan will come home late tonight. He hath a meeting."

"Sounds fine to me. I hope you feel better soon. Where are we going?"

"To the library. I want to know if Martha and Allen liked the ranch, um, home they were going to thee—er, look at."

She was trying to avoid ess words and prevent lisping. I grinned, but didn't say anything about it. "Library's fine with me."

We reached the library in a minute or two, parked the car in a shady spot, and walked on in. Martha McNair sat at the front desk, as usual, and smiled when she saw us.

We walked on over to the desk and all greeted each other. "How wath your trip to the ranch? The old one?" Janet shot me a despairing glance and I picked up her question full of esses. "The old ranch house for sale that you and Allen were going to see on Sunday. Did you like it?"

Martha brightened up. "Oh, we did. It's really nice, very suitable, and Allen's interested in renovating it. He's drawing some plans and estimating the costs. If it turns out okay, we'll make an offer on it, just a little bit less than the asking price. I like the house and the idea of living in the country. I'm hoping it all works out."

"Great!" said Janet. "I hope it workth, um, workth out for you."

"We were glad our real estate agent met us there. He knew a lot about the property, and reassured us when we took a look at the small barn. Apparently someone has been staying there. There was a small room in one corner of the barn, and there we saw a sleeping bag and an ice cooler with food that won't spoil easily. Maybe a hunter stays there overnight now and then, but it could be someone who would vandalize the house. I'd hate to see that happen."

"My goodness! What did you do?"

"Carl Jennings, our agent, said he'd report it to the sheriff's department so they could deal with it. I'm not sure what's been done, though I want it to be taken care of before we go back to take a second look."

"Tell that to Carl Jennings and he'll take care of it," I said with certainty. A real estate agent's desire to sell a ranch house would motivate him to clear the barn of any hunters or hobos occupying it. My mother had been a real estate agent in Houston, and I'd learned a thing or two about the business.

"I'll call him again," Martha said. "Oh, by the way, your cousin Lisa and her band will be here next Monday afternoon. They're going to play three sets, each one a selection of early country songs. Classes from the elementary school can walk over here to our auditorium, and with three sets we can accommodate all the students." She beamed, and I could tell she looked forward to her special project.

"Maybe I can write a newspaper column about it," I said. "My first column will appear tomorrow in the Yorktown *Chronicle*. It's sort of an introduction of myself. Anyway, I think the editor would approve of a column covering music performed for our children. Is it okay if Janet and I attend?"

"Of course!" Martha was excited at the idea. "I'll save you some chairs where the teachers sit, and anything else I can do, just let me know."

"It's a deal." We shook hands on it and laughed.

Janet had found some books to check out and was ready to go. We stopped at Dairy Queen and ordered an ice cream cone for each of us. The soft ice cream soothed Janet's hunger pangs, but it didn't need to be chewed. While she ate her ice cream, I asked Janet to drive us over to Aunt Hettie's house. "I have some questions I'd like to ask her, things she might know and be persuaded to discuss."

Janet nodded, and soon we were on our way. We reached Aunt Hettie's house a little after four and found her on the front porch sipping iced tea. Donny had gone somewhere on his motorcycle and Aunt Hettie had just returned from the grocery store. Her Oldsmobile stood by the front gate of the chain-link fence.

Aunt Hettie had already unloaded some of the bags of groceries. The store clerk had placed those items going into the refrigerator or freezer into lightweight packages, while heavier bags of cans, washer detergent, sacks of sugar and flour, waited for Donny to carry them in.

"We'll carry those things inside for you," Janet and I told Aunt Hettie. "Do you know when Donny will get home?"

"Oh, he won't be gone too long. Have a seat here on the porch with me. There's a pitcher of iced tea in the kitchen if you want to get some first."

Janet and I looked at each other. The afternoon temperature had shot up, and iced tea on the front porch suddenly seemed perfect.

"Thank you. We'll get some and be back in a minute."

"Bring me some more, too, would you?" Aunt Hettie handed me her empty glass. She looked too comfortable in her rocking chair to get up and go to the kitchen herself, and she'd slipped off her shoes. She was rocking the chair with her bare feet.

I took her empty glass to the kitchen and filled it first with ice and sweet tea, then Janet and I each fixed a glass for ourselves.

We returned to the porch, gave Aunt Hettie her second glass of tea, and pulled chairs for ourselves close to hers. The porch roof shaded us, and a nice breeze cooled us from the afternoon warm temperature.

I took a deep drink of my iced tea, and then took a deep breath. Aunt Hettie looked quiet, calm, and peaceful. I took another deep breath.

"Aunt Hettie," Janet said, "Caroline would like to ask you some questions about our family history. Is that all right with you?"

Janet's lisp had finally disappeared, and I appreciated her helping me. Aunt Hettie was not disturbed by the request. "Sure," she said. "Fire away."

Firing away wasn't what I meant to do; I just wanted to ask about the rifle. "Aunt Hettie, I read last week's *Chronicle* again this morning, and I noticed the description of the rifle Danny was holding when his photograph was taken. A Henry .44 from the 1850s, it was called. Is that something you keep here in your house?"

"Oh, yes. It's in the gun rack in my bedroom. My great-aunt passed it down to me when I was just a little girl and she was a very old lady."

"Where did the rifle come from?" I asked. "Who first owned it, and how did your great-aunt come to possess it?"

"It first belonged to John David Hargrove, who bought it for use during the Civil War. It was a new invention then, and lots of Yankee soldiers used it, but only a few in the Confederate Army used it if they had access to its special ammunition. Some of the Texas units did, but most did not. I keep other old rifles in my gun rack, too. Some were used during the early days of the colony, and the Texas revolution to get free from Mexico, and during the days before the Civil War."

She took a sip of her iced tea and was quiet for a minute. "Caroline Jane learned how to shoot with some of those guns, and they're what she and Willie used for hunting and fighting during the Civil War, when John David was fighting the Civil War with the Henry."

"What happened to the Henry rifle when the war was over?"

"By then, the Henry rifle was popular. Eventually it would turn into the Winchester rifle, but after the war, John David bought a new one for himself and gave his old one to Caroline Jane."

"What! You're kidding me."

"No, I'm not." Aunt Hettie rocked herself back and forth for a few minutes. "This happened when Caroline Jane was preparing to marry James Jamison and move to the new ranch. John David knew she'd use a rifle for hunting and protection, just like she always had. She was a very good shot. Today, she'd be out there winning hunting trophies. But in her day, when she got married, the best thing her father could give her was a good rifle for hunting and self-defense."

Aunt Hettie continued, "She used the rifle on the ranch many times when her husband was gone on a vigilante raid. He wasn't there to protect her, or hunt for food they needed. She took the rifle with her to Arizona, too. It eventually came back to Texas after she died in Tucson. Priscilla Gaines took charge of it then, but she didn't know how to use it."

So she knew about Priscilla, and a lot of family history all together. Her age, knowledge and memory made her an excellent source of information. "Why did Caroline Jane go to Arizona?" I asked. "Her husband had disappeared. At our family meeting, pretty much everyone finally agreed he's the second body in Thomas Watson Hargrove's grave, though they're not sure who shot him. Anyway, with her husband gone, why didn't Caroline Jane go back to her ranch and find another husband?"

Aunt Hettie's eyes were half closed, and she gave a sardonic chuckle. "I was wondering if you'd ask that question."

"Do you know the answer?"

"I do. I've kept the secret for many years, ever since my great-aunt gave me the rifle and told me why. Very few other people knew, and they have passed away. I doubt that anyone else knows but me."

I held my breath and waited for her to continue. Janet's eyes were big as saucers, and she held her breath too.

After a minute, Aunt Hettie said, "I'm going to tell you what happened, and leave its secrecy up to you. It might be time to tell the truth about what happened in 1875. Who'd go to jail for it now?"

"Go to jail? For what?"

"For shooting her husband, that's what. Caroline Jane's the one who did that, not her father or brothers."

"What! How could she do that? The family men were waiting for James Jamison at the crossroad near their house, to protect Caroline Jane. They were going to warn Jamison off and send him home, but it turned into a shooting instead."

"Well, Caroline Jane pulled the trigger. She took her rifle and laid in wait farther up the road than the men. When Jamison showed up, she called out to him to send him away, but he turned toward her and pulled out his gun. She shot him with her rifle."

"Oh, my God. Did she get caught? Did her relatives know?"

"Of course. The men at the crossroad heard the shot and galloped their horses toward it. They found Caroline Jane with Jamison's body on the ground. His horse had run away. Caroline Jane took his hand gun and his gold watch and threw them into a huge patch of cactus. The rest of the story is familiar. Caroline Jane's brothers and father took her husband's body and put it in the grave prepared for her grandfather who was dying."

Janet and I both sat stunned, trying to absorb the information.

"So Jamison's death and burial were a family secret, and if any accusations were made, they were denied and the grave was guarded against being dug up."

"That's right."

"So, once again—why was the professor digging up the grave? Did he think he could prove something, or what? And how far did he think he could get with a camping shovel?"

"I don't know," Aunt Hettie said. "If I'd known what he was going to do, I would never have taken him to our family cemetery. And I don't know who shot him, either. It wasn't me, and if I knew who did, I wouldn't keep it a secret."

Another sip of iced tea emptied her glass. "I've told you what I do know. It's a relief, and I'm surprised. It's as if a burden has rolled off my shoulders."

The three of us sat in silence, each thinking things over.

124

Cemetery Whites

Janet pointed to her wristwatch. Clearly, she was thinking it was time for dinner.

We said goodbye to Aunt Hettie. "Thanks for the iced tea, and thank you very much for telling us about Caroline Jane and the Henry rifle."

"Oh, you're welcome," Aunt Hettie said. "I enjoyed our visit. Come back soon, and I'll show you how to shoot. You might need to do it yourself someday."

We drove to Casa Rosa for a Mexican dinner. Janet said enchiladas would be easier for her to chew than anything served at Stockman's. After we ordered, our dinners appeared very soon on the table.

"Are you going to write about Caroline Jane in next week's column?" she asked me, tackling her steaming enchiladas.

"Oh, no. Maybe never. You know, I think a trip to San Antonio tomorrow would be a good thing to do. Do you want to go?"

"I guess so. I can drive us there again. What are we going to do?"

"I'll call David and see if we can have lunch with him. I'd like to report what we've turned up so far as the family's amateur detectives, and I'd rather do that in person than on the phone. Before lunch, we might have time to visit the Ellis area—what's left of it. That's where Willie lived, and his mother moved in with him when she returned from Tucson. That's where they raised the orphan Priscilla had taken in while she was staying with Tom in Arizona. I'm curious about the boy's schooling. He must have had some kind of education that enabled him to do so well in business. What was available in San Antonio in the late 1800s? I didn't see anything about it in the Gaines family booklet."

"Sounds fine to me." Janet rolled up a tortilla, spreading a spoonful of beans on it first. "You know, I'm learning a lot more about things than I used to. I like driving us around. Who knows what we'll discover next?"

She smiled, and I laughed. "I couldn't get around without you,"

Connie Knight

I said. "The roads out here still run in circles for me."

"Oh, they'll unravel eventually. Meantime, I'll drive. Want me to pick you up tomorrow?"

"Sure. Is nine o'clock okay? We could have a quick breakfast here, if you want, before we hit the road."

"Sounds fine." Janet raised her cup of coffee. "Let's toast to a good day tomorrow."

We clicked our coffee cups together and drank the coffee as if it were wine.

After dinner, Janet drove me home. Instead of reviewing any more letters, I called David and set up lunch for one o'clock.

Then I got my pen and papers and made a list of things to discuss with him.

CHAPTER THIRTEEN
Wednesday, March 24, 2010

Janet and I were waiting for our *huevos a la Mexicana* by nine-fifteen on Wednesday. I had my pens, pad of paper, and list of items to discuss with David, but the new issues of Yorktown *Chronicle* were stacked on the table near the cash register. Janet and I put the David agenda aside and took copies of the newspaper so we could read my column. Everybody else in the restaurant was reading the newspaper, too.

They must have read my column, because they looked at me and seemed curious, but only our waitress raised a question. Aricela brought a tray to our table, slid the steaming plates to their positions in front of us, and then pointed to the newspaper I had set down. It was opened and folded to show my photograph and column so I could read it.

"That you?" Aricela asked, pointing at the photo.

I nodded and smiled. Aricela smiled back, then raised her head and looked at everybody else in the room. "It's her," she called out. "Just like we thought; it's her."

There were a dozen other people in the restaurant. They smiled at me, some applauded, and some called, "Welcome!"

"Thank you!" I managed to call in response, and then shrank as far as I could into the corner of our booth.

"Oh, don't be embarrassed," chided Janet. "Your column was very nice and well-received. You opened your heart, and nobody's holding anything against you."

"There's one who might," I muttered. In the far corner of the room, Henry Hargrove's white hair and wrinkled face had become apparent. He was looking at me, not in a very friendly way.

I tried to ignore him and eat my Mexican-style scrambled eggs in peace and quiet. Things were smoothing out. Then into the restaurant walked Gregory Jackson.

He approached our booth. "Mind if I join you?" he asked, and sat beside Janet so he could stare at me. "I read your column. You're a good writer, better than I am in some ways. The dissertation I'm working on is an arrangement of data researched for a certain era. Underneath, it's interesting, but the format for proving my thesis is pretty dry."

"Thanks," I said. "It's a surprise to see you here, Gregory. I thought by now you'd be back at the university, working as a teaching assistant and finishing your dissertation."

"Ha, ha. So did I, but the new teaching assistant job hasn't materialized yet, and neither has the replacement for Professor Harrison to be my mentor. I'm spending a lot of time here researching county records. Looking for some things to polish and complete what I'm writing."

"Did you attend Professor Harrison's funeral?" I asked him. "I thought I saw you there."

Gregory handed his menu back to Aricela. "Eggs like theirs, and some coffee, too."

Aricela served him a cup of coffee, and Gregory added cream, no sugar. "I went to the funeral," he said. "I saw the two of you at the reception after the burial, but you disappeared before I had a chance to say hello."

I should have kept my mouth shut, but I didn't foresee Gregory's reaction. "Oh, we were in a meeting with Estelle Shawn. We told her about finding the professor's body and calling the police. Other things, too. She gave us a Gaines family tree booklet. Some pieces of information it contained, linked with some things I'd found out recently, were so amazing. It showed how the Harrisons were connected to the Gaineses, who had worked for the

Hargroves as slaves and then as freedmen! Before that, I didn't understand why Professor Harrison would be interested in the Hargrove cemetery. In fact, I still don't understand what he was doing with his shovel. However, Estelle gave us copies of old letters and documents that were in the attic, things she said her brother never knew existed..." I babbled on, more and more nervous, because Gregory's expression became more and more angry about what I said.

"She gave things to you that she withheld from her brother! For God's sake, he wouldn't have known as much as he did if it hadn't been for my research! And now, when someone else at the university will become my mentor, well, that person may not take so much interest in my research as Professor Harrison did. To think what might be in those letters, and I didn't have access to them."

"They're letters about Caroline Jane Jamison's trip to Arizona with her brother. Priscilla Gaines accompanied her, but Caroline Jane got sick and died, and Priscilla returned to Texas." I didn't feel like going into more detail. Gregory's face was bright red, and his eyes glared.

Worse yet, Henry Hargrove was at the cash register, near our booth, and he heard what we were saying. His own face turned red and his eyes glared, too.

"You went to that man's funeral!" he sputtered at me. "What do you think he was doing in a white family's cemetery? Digging for gold, that's what! Some kind of treasure he knows about, but won't share with anybody else."

"You're right about that," Gregory said. "He was a greedy, ambitious man. That's what got him into gambling debt, and motivated him into pushing me so hard for researching his family. I did a lot of work on his family project, even though it didn't have much to do with my *Pee Aitch Dee!*"

Janet and I put some money on the table. We left our breakfasts half-finished, scrambled out of the booth and headed for the door.

Henry Hargrove and Gregory Jackson were still glaring at each other and arguing about the merits of Harrison's family history. We could see them through the windows as we jumped into the maroon sedan and fastened our seat belts. Aricela's father, Juan Ramos, owner of the restaurant, walked toward the old man and the young man on the verge of fighting with each other.

"Oh, oh. They're on their way out," Janet said. She switched the car's ignition on and geared it into reverse. We backed out of the parking space and headed toward the road.

As we left the parking lot, we could see Henry and Gregory exiting the restaurant, escorted by Mr. Ramos. They were still arguing, but not in the restaurant.

"I'm glad you didn't tell Gregory what Aunt Hettie told us," Janet said. "Talk about a rooster fight! Those two were getting into one, weren't they?"

"Getting into something somehow." I thought about the two of them for a while. "Somehow they seem a lot alike. Gregory looks and acts like a young version of old Henry. You don't think we're related to the Jacksons somehow, do you?"

"We all go back to Adam and Eve. Research it and you might find something somewhere."

I considered her comment. "Next time I see him, I'll ask him," I said. "With all his research, he must have checked into his own family tree along the way."

"For God's sake, yes!" Janet said, using Gregory's tone of voice. We both giggled and then moved on to a different topic of conversation.

"We're almost in San Antonio, and lunch with David isn't until one o'clock. Do you know the way to Ellis Alley?"

"I know it's on the east side of downtown. Can you take the map from the glove compartment and navigate?"

I did, and soon we were looking for Ellis Alley. The map showed a tiny road intersecting with Chestnut Street between East Commerce and Houston Street. We drove around and around, looking for the tiny restored Ellis Alley neighborhood I'd read about. The area was quiet, just blocks away from Dignowity Park to the north and the Alamodome to the south. Off Chestnut Street, there were vacant lots and commercial buildings; to the north were residential streets with old houses.

Finally we parked the car near Chestnut Street and walked over to three old houses facing Chestnut Street. Two of them looked pretty from renovation, and a two-story house next to them looked like it still needed some work. Behind them, on a large lot, stood a huge, towering building with a sign that read, "Condos for Sale".

"This doesn't look like the alley where Willie found a job and a house," I remarked to Janet.

We were approaching the restored old houses, and a black-and-silver metal sign appeared. It read:

THE ELLIS ALLEY ENCLAVE

The houses preserved as the Ellis Alley Enclave are what remain of one of the first settlements of African Americans in San Antonio after Emancipation.

Dr. Anthony Dignowity and Samuel Maverick acquired most of a Spanish land grant area, the sign continued. *By the late 1860s, the land was being developed, and was racially mixed. By 1879, 25-foot lots were purchased solely by African Americans. In the first decades of the 20th Century, Ellis Alley became the neighborhood from which the "Black East Side" of San Antonio evolved. Eventually, the neighborhoods farther east became more desirable and the Ellis Alley area lost its stability.*

We read the sign silently.

"I guess we won't find any traces of Willie here," Janet said.

"Guess not." I showed Janet the San Antonio map. "See the bare spots with no streets? They're occupied by the Hemisphere Park with all its buildings, and the Alamodome with its parking lots.

Blocks of old houses were razed to make space for them, beginning in the sixties. The area over here didn't get totally razed, but not completely salvaged, either."

Silence held us for another few minutes.

"At least these buildings have been saved," I said. One served as a dentist's office, and the other dealt out bus schedules and tickets for the Metropolitan Transit. According to the sign, a partnership between VIA Metropolitan Transit, the City of San Antonio, Neighborhoods Acting Together, and the San Antonio Conservation Society restored the buildings. *Bless them for saving some of what was once here*, I thought.

"It's almost time to drive to Schilo's, isn't it?" Janet asked.

She was right. We walked back to the car and took another look at the map. Schilo's wasn't far away, but we'd have to find a place to park.

We were lucky. We found a space in a little parking lot around the block from Schilo's, and the short walk to the restaurant took us along the San Antonio River, the beautiful water threading its way through downtown.

I remembered Schilo's from previous trips to San Antonio. I always loved to go there. The old restaurant, founded in 1917 by a German family, flourished in its current location since 1942. It occupied a large room with delicatessen cases along one side of the room, showing off fancy foods. Along the back of the room, a bar served beer and wine. Along the far side, tall-backed booths made of old dark wood provide a comfortable place to sit. Large tables of dark wood occupied the center of the room. The ceiling is covered with old pressed tin squares, and tiles decorate the floor.

We found seats in one of the booths, and the waitress delivered our menus. They still served the famous split pea soup created by Mama Schilo during the Depression. I decided to order Polska Kielbasa with a cup of soup. Janet was still studying the menu when David joined us.

David was genial, authoritative. He welcomed us to San

Antonio, suggested items on the menu, and ordered lunch for us when the waitress arrived. While we waited for our food, I put my paper pad on the table. "I made a list of things to discuss," I told David, and added, "I'm the one who volunteered to be the family's amateur detective, but really, Janet and I have worked together on almost everything. We did something almost every day."

"Well, let's see what you, I mean both of you, have discovered." David looked at my list. "Wow," he said. "This is a lot."

The list included working with Great-Aunt Hettie and Donny, finding her Colt .45 bullet, meeting with Constable Bob Bennett, and hearing that someone else had shot a Glock bullet, which was fatal. It covered attending the rooster fight and talking to the bookie about a hit man for the professor's gambling debts, which he denied.

There was the possibility of a racist, like Henry Hargrove, having taken the random opportunity of shooting the black professor (unlikely—not enough people roaming around the country).

What other culprits could there be? With his teaching assistant, Gregory Jackson, we had discussed the professor's life, and had attended his funeral, where we talked with his sister. We didn't find anyone, and neither have the DeWitt County police.

The last item on the list read:

Second corpse in grave—question resolved. Source: Great-Aunt Hettie

James Jamison was shot by his wife who had left him. He wanted to retrieve her, but she didn't want to go back to the ranch with him. He pulled a gun on her, and she shot him with her Henry rifle.

David read the list and asked questions, which I answered in some detail. Finally he got to the last item, and read it aloud incredulously.

Connie Knight

"Is this *serious*? Wow! I can hardly believe it."

"I believe what Aunt Hettie told us," Janet told him, standing up for me. "She told us more than is written there. To prove it, we could dig up the corpse and identify the bullet of Caroline Jane's rare Henry rifle."

"Well, we're not going to dig up the grave. Don't even think about that. The family has resisted that for more than a century. Still—you think Aunt Hettie knows the truth?"

"She said so. Said she's the only person still alive who ever heard the story. Said she heard it from an old aunt when she was a young girl," Janet said.

"Said that's how she heard about the Henry rifle, too," I added. "In my opinion, the old person who told her was probably Sarah Gaines Hargrove, Caroline Jane's mother."

"Well, I'm impressed," David said. "It's been just a week since the family meeting and you've found out quite a lot. Aunt Hettie really pulled a gun on Professor Harrison?"

"Yes, because he was digging up the grave. She didn't want that either. At first she thought her bullet had killed him, even though by accident. But Bob Bennett had told me about the Glock bullet, so Janet and I visited Aunt Hettie, and she and Donny agreed to talk to Bob Bennett about it."

"You must have made a good impression on her. She really said that about Caroline Jane?"

I explained about the years of hunting and fighting, especially during the Civil War when the men were gone. "Willie Gaines helped her with that. He was a slave a couple of years older than her, and they did a lot of farm and ranch work together. That's something else we discovered. The Harrison family is a branch of the black Gaines family. They're descended from an orphan adopted and raised by Willie and his mother Priscilla. She, along with her husband who died, and their son Willie, were sent to Texas with Sarah Gaines when she married John David Hargrove."

"Wow."

Cemetery Whites

"There's a lot I didn't write down. I'm interested in our family history, and I've been reading old documents. Cousin Miranda gave me copies of letters she has collected, and Estelle Shawn—the professor's sister—had a box of old documents from the Gaines family in her mother's attic. She made copies for us, and I've been reading them."

" Found any new things out?'

"Not new exactly. The interesting thing is that any letters from Caroline Jane are missing. Maybe they've been collected elsewhere. Could be sitting in somebody else's attic."

"Well—wow." David finished his glass of beer and glanced at his watch. "I've got to get back to the office pretty soon." He took something out of his suit jacket's inner pocket. "Here's an invitation you might already have received. The historic society has rescued a deteriorated family cemetery in DeWitt County, and they're holding a ceremony tomorrow morning to dedicate it—to history, I guess. You can have the invitation; I can't go. Just call Miranda for directions, and you can ask her to bring any letters she has that you'd want to see."

"Wow," I said. Extending the invitation, David seemed to open a door for me that Miranda hadn't. "Thank you. I'll go."

Schilo's waitress brought us a bill, and David took it. "There's a cash register on the way out. I'll take care of this. Let's see each other again pretty soon, and just give me a call if anything else comes up. Sorry I've got to leave, but there's a meeting."

He took off, and Janet and I stayed in the booth to finish our lunch.

Soon we were on the road home. Janet dropped me off at my cottage. "I'll call you after I talk to Miranda," I told her. "We can make plans for tomorrow then."

She drove off, on her way home, and I let myself into my nice, cool house. I changed into some jeans and a tee shirt, made some coffee and poured myself a cup, then flipped on the TV and settled down in front of it.

Connie Knight

"Wow," I muttered, thinking of David and his response to my list of things accomplished. Of course, there was still more to do, and I liked that. I'd rather have things to do than sit around the house all the time—like I did in Houston after I retired.

I finished the coffee at leisure, muted the TV, and picked up the phone from the little table next to the sofa. The invitation was there, too. I opened it and dialed Miranda's phone number.

She answered promptly. "Hello?"

"Hi, Miranda, this is Caroline Hamilton. Remember me? You gave me a stack of documents a couple of months ago, and I've been going through them."

I told her about the letters I got from Estelle and offered to bring copies to her. She was excited. "The only thing is, letters to or from Caroline Jane are missing. Someone must have culled them out. Do you happen to have any?" I held my breath, waiting for her reply.

"No, I don't," Miranda said. "In fact, I don't know much about her. She left Texas and moved West, so I haven't followed her. There are so many relatives here, I spend my time on them."

"Well, I'll bring you what I have. Are you attending the cemetery dedication tomorrow morning?"

"The Owens family place that's been restored? Yes, I am. It's pretty far off the road, though. Close to where the original Owens ranch house used to be. I don't know if you could find it easily."

"Oh, Janet will drive us," I said blithely. "A map came with the invitation, too. So we can meet there tomorrow."

"There's one other thing to look for," Miranda said. "A herd of javelinas lives close to the cemetery. That's why we put up a chain-link fence. It protects the cemetery, and protected us, too, while we were working on it."

"Oooh. Did they bother you? I've heard they can be dangerous."

"No, they left us alone, but you're right. They can be dangerous. Their tusks are sharp as razors. Just watch out, and stay away from

136

them."

"Thanks for the warning. Janet and I will see you tomorrow then."

I called Janet to tell her about the map, the wild hogs, and the chain-link fence. "Pick me up at nine and go to breakfast?"

"Sure. The ceremony's at eleven, isn't it? We'll have plenty of time to find it using the map."

We hung up and went on our ways. Bob was taking me to dinner, so I changed into some slacks and a nicer shirt, put on a little makeup, and watched the news on TV until the door bell rang at seven.

It was Bob. I grabbed my purse and we drove to Stockman's. I smiled at Bob, thinking how nice it was to go out for breakfast, lunch, and dinner so frequently instead of cooking at home and washing dishes every single day. I didn't say it out loud, though. Just smiled.

We found our table at the restaurant, settled in, and ordered dinner. Then I told Bob about the day. Gregory Jackson and Henry Hargrove at breakfast, David at lunch, and the javelina-ridden invitation to a cemetery ceremony tomorrow morning.

"Aren't you forgetting something?"

"What did I forget?"

"Your column. Your first column printed today."

"Oh, my goodness, you're right. Oh! I forgot to give a copy of it to David today."

"Well, I got a copy, and I read it. I thought it was good. Very good."

I could have kissed him in public, but I refrained. "Why, thank you, Bob. I'll be writing one every week, and maybe some free-lance articles too, so you'll have more of my work to read. Oh! I forgot to tell you about Caroline Jane and the Henry rifle. I'll write a column about it someday, but not yet. This is still a secret, okay?"

I proceeded to tell him the truth about the second corpse, and how I'd found it out.

"Your Great-Aunt Hettie knows a lot," Bob mused. "Maybe more than she's telling us about the death of Harrison. What do you think?"

I shook my head. "I asked her, and she said she didn't know."

"I sure wish she did. Even a clue would help. We haven't found anything out, not even anything about the Glock."

"There's something Henry Hargrove said. He said it twice, actually. Once when we encountered him in the cemetery, and again this morning in the restaurant when he overheard us talking about Professor Harrison. Each time, he made a reference to treasure or gold that Harrison could have been digging for. Nobody else said that. Everyone thought Harrison's digging had something to do with the second body."

"If Henry really thought there might be treasure, don't you think he might have already dug it up himself?"

I shrugged. "I don't know. He's odd. Anyway, I'm just repeating what he said. I don't know any more than that."

"Hmm. Well, maybe I can talk to him tomorrow. I'm working late, remember. I'll follow your Uncle Cotton's wolf hunt; maybe Henry will attend. Or I'll find him at home."

"I'd sure like to know what you find out."

"Oh, I'll tell you whatever I find out. We can have dinner again on Friday, and I have the weekend off too."

That sounded good to me.

Dinner was soon over. Bob drove me home and came inside for a while. We watched TV—a show and the news. Just like last time, he put his arm around me and pulled me close, and I leaned up against him. It was soothing, reassuring, and romantic.

At ten-thirty, I walked him to the front porch door and he kissed me goodnight. "See you Friday," he said, and I whispered, "Okay." He whistled a tune as he walked to his car. Something cheerful, which is how I felt. I closed the door and got myself ready for bed.

Cemetery Whites

CHAPTER FOURTEEN
Thursday, March 25, 2010

Janet picked me up at nine o'clock and we drove to Casa Rosa for breakfast. Ariela waited on us, as usual, and we ordered the same *huevos a la Mexicana*, one with peppers and one without. We complimented each other on the nice clothes we wore for the Owens cemetery dedication. Janet's red woolen jacket and patent leather shoes stood out especially.

In the restaurant, the only difference between yesterday and today was the absence of Henry Hargrove and Gregory Jackson. Juan Ramos came over to our table to apologize for their behavior.

Janet consoled him. "What they did was not your fault. We saw you taking them outside after we left the restaurant and got into our car. I'm sure everyone in here felt better after they were gone."

"You think so?" Mr. Ramos brightened up. "Well, they won't be coming back here. I told them they are banned from this restaurant. Funny thing is, after I threw them out and scolded them, they stopped fighting. They got in the same car and left together."

Aricela Ramos, Juan's daughter, arrived at the table with our eggs. "I saw them together at the Dairy Queen last night. Wayne Martin took me there for some ice cream, and those two guys were eating hamburgers and French fries. Dinner, if you ask me."

"What were you doing with Wayne Martin? I thought you were rehearsing with the choir at the church."

"Papa! I was with the choir for rehearsing. So was Wayne. He just invited me for an ice cream sundae when rehearsal was over, and then he drove me home."

"Mary Louise was supposed to drive you home...." Father and daughter drifted away from our table. A kinder, gentler argument than yesterday's was developing. Janet and I finished our breakfast, left money on the table, and headed for the parking lot, just like we did before.

So Henry and Gregory had dinner together at the Dairy Queen last night. I puzzled over their sudden friendship, or research association, while Janet drove us to the library. I wondered what the twosome could have been thinking. Did old Henry Hargrove know about Caroline Jane and the Henry rifle? Would that be of any interest to Gregory?

"Here we are," Janet announced, breaking my reverie. She'd found a parking place in front of the library. Soon we were inside, looking for Martha at the front counter.

We were happy to see each other. Martha had something to tell us, and we had the Gaines family tree booklet for her. She let us go first, admired the booklet, and promised to set up a Gaines folder in the file cabinet behind her counter.

"It gives me a place to keep donated documents that pertain to local families and their history. You might want to look through it sometime. There're all kinds of information."

I found the idea intriguing, but Janet brushed it aside. "We won't have time today. We're going to the dedication of the Owens historic family cemetery near here, and we'll need time to drive around and find it. It's pretty far off the road, according to the map that came with our invitation."

"Map to a cemetery?" Martha was surprised. "That's the thing I was going to tell you about. A young man from San Antonio was here earlier this morning, and that's what he wanted. A map to the cemetery dedication. He'd heard about it, but I guess he didn't have a formal invitation including a map. Anyway, he copied some pages from our book on historic cemeteries. That book's been popular lately! It's the same one Professor Harrison looked at, and you, too, Caroline, if you remember."

Cemetery Whites

"Maybe we'll see him at the cemetery, along with the members of the historic society. What's his name?" I asked.

"I don't know his name. He'll be easy to identify, though. He's black, probably in his early twenties; tall, thin, real nice looking, in my opinion. Nicely dressed, I guess for the ceremony."

"Did he wear gold-rimmed glasses? Did he have short hair and a moustache?" I was almost certain the cemetery visitor would be Josh Gaines.

"Yes, that sounds like him. Do you know him from somewhere?"

"We met him at his cousin's funeral. I bumped into him by accident, and it really offended him at first. I hope he's over it by now. His name is Josh Gaines, and he's related to Professor Harrison—second cousin once removed, something like that."

"Maybe he'll be a little more polite," Janet piped up. "I hate to put an end to this visit, but we'd better get going if we want to be on time."

"Please let me know what you find out. I'm interested," Martha said. Other library patrons were approaching the counter with books to check out, so she turned toward them and we turned toward the door.

Once on the road, I pulled the map out of my purse and looked at it for navigation. "At first, we head toward the dirt road that goes by the ranch house for sale and then Bob's house. Then we turn on a road past that. This ought to be pretty easy. Piece of cake!"

I relaxed, confident in finding our way. The roadsides displayed colorful drifts of blooming wildflowers, primarily bluebonnets, with other swaths of pink, yellow and white. Behind the fences, there were fields of green grass and grazing cattle. We turned onto the familiar dirt road and drove on, passing the house for sale and then Bob's house. Soon after, we were heading through land that was not cleared and green. Most of it was covered with brush, at least near the fences and the road. At last we came to a right-turn road. There was no sign to identify it, but it compared with the map. "This must be it," I told Janet. "It looks right to me."

Janet consulted the map and agreed. "If we can't find the cemetery, we'll just turn around and go back. We'll try the next road if this one doesn't work."

We made the turn and soon ran up to a gate, closed and blocking the road. It wasn't locked, though. I got out and opened the gate; Janet drove through; I closed the gate and hopped back into the car. I noticed a padlock and a chain on the ground by the gate; maybe someone had taken them off and set them aside for the cemetery dedication crowd.

We drove on and on. The car's speed was slower and slower and the road became narrower and rougher. Potholes began to appear. Finally we came to a muddy spot, a huge pothole that blocked the road. Janet put the brakes on, and the car stopped short of the pothole.

"What now?" I asked. My mind and my map were blank. Maybe Janet knew what to do next; I didn't.

We had reached a stretch of land covered with grass and patches of prickly pear cactus. Tall trees grew here and there, but you could see farther than in the brush-covered area. Finally Janet said, "Let's get out and see if we could drive around this pothole. Maybe there will be some tire tracks we can follow."

She opened her door and got out of the car, walking gingerly in her patent leather shoes. We'd both dressed up for the ceremony. Janet's clothes included a red wool jacket, black trousers, and red patent leather shoes. I wore a navy blue jacket with matching pants and black leather loafers for comfort. When I got out of the car, I walked even more slowly than Janet.

"What's that smell?" My nose wrinkled as we approached the pothole.

Suddenly I saw the answer to my question. From a patch of mesquite brush and prickly pear, maybe a hundred feet away, emerged a huge javelina, his ivory razor-sharp tusks glinting in the sunlight. His family of five or six more followed him, heading

142

toward their pothole.

Maybe they didn't see us yet, but they would soon. Too soon. "Janet!" I called softly, but she didn't hear me. She was on the other side of the car, pretty far away, walking and looking for car tracks. "Janet!" I shrieked. "Some javelinas are here."

By that time, I was running back to the car. I got in and slammed the door. Janet must have heard my shout, and felt too far away from the car. She was close to a middle-sized tree with some branches sagging to the ground. She ran to the tree, leaped into it, and climbed from one branch to another. Soon she was close to the top.

The javelina leader had seen her and run for her, but she was high in the tree before he reached it. Her leather shoes had fallen to the ground, and the huge wild hog began eating them.

"Caroline!" Janet shouted. She was looking for me; she didn't know I was in her maroon sedan. I clambered over into the driver's seat, rolled the window down, and called to her. "Janet! I'm over here. I'm in the car."

I waved out the window and she saw me. The javelina had settled down under her tree, still chewing on her discarded shoes. His herd had scattered, but he seemed set on staying where he was.

"Janet! What are we going to do?" I wailed, calling loudly enough so she could hear me.

"My key is in the car, isn't it?"

I looked. It was still in the ignition.

"Want me to start the engine and honk the horn? Try to scare them away?"

"No! I'm not getting out of this tree until they're gone for good. If you just scare them, they might turn around and run back before I can get in the car."

I didn't think that was too likely, but I could understand why Janet didn't want to take the chance.

"I've got an idea," she called. "You can drive my car, can't you? Just turn around and go back to the road. Somebody ought to pass

Connie Knight

by pretty soon. Just get some help and come get me. Does your cell phone work?"

"No. We must be out of the zone."

"If nobody passes by in an hour, you'll have to drive back to the paved road. The cell phones work there, and you can call for help. Call Jordan, or Bob Bennett—whoever you can get. If somebody from the cemetery dedication passes by, I'll ask them to stay with me, but I'm not getting out of this tree until I'm sure it's safe."

I'd never heard Janet speak so adamantly about anything, but she presented her plan with certainty.

"Okay," I called to her. "I'll do it if that's what you want. Sounds like it might take a couple of hours, though."

"That's okay. Better safe than sorry."

I settled into the driver's seat and switched the engine on. The car turned around easily on the narrow road. I tooted the horn to tell Janet goodbye, then drove off at a slow, bouncing pace, following the potholed road we had taken on our way in.

Not that the road was that easy to follow. In some places, it was narrow and obscure, like a trail instead of a road, and I was afraid I'd turn in a wrong direction. Thank goodness for the bright sunlight; in dawn or twilight, I was sure I'd lose the way. I drove slowly, and the series of potholes looked like those we had crossed heading in the opposite direction. They weren't real landmarks, though. There weren't any. The ranch seemed unattended. Grass and weeds, brushy trees, and patches of prickly pear abounded, and they all looked the same to me.

Eventually the road became wider and more distinct. After a while, I could see a gate in the distance. I headed for it, more hopeful every minute. Once there, I hopped out of the car and opened the gate. The chain and padlock, I noticed, were still lying on the ground. That worried me. What if somebody closed the gate and put the chain and padlock in place? How could Janet's rescuer, along with me, get through the gate and follow the potholed road? I prudently picked up the chain and padlock and put them in the car.

144

I'd return them when Janet, rescuer, and I were on our way out.

Back in the car, I drove down the rest of the ranch road and stopped the car when it reached the county dirt road. Which way to turn? If I turned left, the road would take me to Bob's house, then the old ranch house for sale. Probably nobody was home. Bob was working, and the old ranch house was empty. I'd have to keep driving back into Yorktown and find a rescuer there, but at least I wouldn't get lost. I was pretty sure I could find the way.

If I turned right, I might find someone more quickly, but what if I took a wrong turn and ended up going around in circles? I didn't know that part of the road. Heads or tails; left or right? I pondered the question and chose left. Outcome, I thought, was more predictable.

I turned left and chugged along in Janet's maroon sedan, soon passing Bob's house. There was no car in the driveway; Bob must be working in his office or on another road. I stopped the car and checked my cell phone. It worked. I called Bob, but he didn't answer, so I left a message about Janet in the tree and me on the road. We need help, call me!

A few miles past Bob's place, there was the old ranch house for sale. I slowed the car down, approaching the place where a gap in the trees allowed a look at the old barn from the road.

A truck! Someone had parked a little red truck behind the barn, which made it visible from the segment of the road where I had stopped.

Who would park behind the barn, I wondered. Most people would park in front of it, where the driveway from the house led. If someone was trying to hide, it was probably whoever had the sleeping bag and box of food in the barn. Probably a hunter. A hobo wouldn't have a truck to park.

Or it could be a real estate agent, a surveyor or appraiser, or an interested buyer like Martha and Allen.

I decided to drive up to the barn, situate the car so I could turn around and speed away if necessary, and then notify the truck owner of my presence. I'd call hello, or honk the horn. Hopefully, I'd get some help in rescuing Janet.

I turned onto the driveway. As I approached the front of the barn, I saw a car parked there, instead of in the back like the truck. I pulled up next to the car and rolled down my window.

"Helloooo the house!" I shouted. I remembered reading about calling out that phrase in the Old West days, when you approached an isolated cabin whose owner might take you for a raider and shoot you.

Nobody answered. "Helloooo the house!" I shouted again, and tooted the horn as well.

The barn door opened by just a crack, and somebody looked out.

"I need some help," I shouted. "Can I talk to you? I'd really appreciate it!"

The barn door opened a little more, and a man's voice called, "Oh, for God's sake, come on in."

I recognized his voice and phrase. "Gregory Jackson!" I shouted happily. "Just the man I'm looking for. I need your help rescuing my cousin Janet."

Gregory opened the barn door wider and stuck his head out, peering at me. "Caroline? Are you Caroline Hamilton?"

I got out of the car and practically skipped toward him at the barn door. "Yes, that's me. I'm Caroline. What are you doing here, Gregory? I thought you'd be back in San Antonio by now."

Gregory opened the door and let me into the barn. It was empty, and the door to the room holding the sleeping bag and food chest was closed. Why did Gregory look so wary? He seemed to mistrust me.

"Aren't you going back to San Antonio pretty soon?" I asked, trying to stimulate a conversation that would make me trustworthy.

"Not yet," he said. "There's still no teaching assistantship, and nobody to mentor the dissertation. Besides that, Estelle Shawn is still trying to evict me from the garage apartment. So I've spent a lot of time here lately, staying at the motel in town, but when this little barn popped up, I decided to stay here sometimes. I have to save money however I can, you know."

I felt sorry for Gregory. "Won't another history professor at the university take you on? Guide you down the road to the Ph. D.?"

"The head of the history department is busy finding other professors to take over Professor Harrison's classes. I guess I'm low on the list, like it or not. Anyway, what were you saying about Janet?"

I told him about the invitation, the map, the potholes, and the javelinas. "She's up in a tree and won't come down until someone is there to chase the wild hogs away. Or shoot them, if that's what it takes. I understand they can be really dangerous."

Suddenly the door to the barn's little room burst open, and out popped Henry Hargrove, showing off the pistol in his hand. "We've got the gun to take care of your problem," he shouted. "She can count on us, can't she, Gregory?"

The closer he came, the stronger the odor of whiskey on his breath. After last night's dinner at the Dairy Queen, he and Gregory must have spent the rest of the evening elsewhere.

Henry Hargrove continued his speech. "You can count on us to help you. We had an argument yesterday at the restaurant, but things became clear and we became friends. We're working on a project together!"

Henry waved the gun with pride, but Gregory's face showed alarm. "Give me my gun, Henry. We don't want it to go off by accident."

"It wouldn't be an accident," Henry huffed. "I can shoot as good as you, handguns or rifles." Outside the open barn door, a sparrow fluttered by. Henry took a quick aim, pulled the trigger, and blew the bird into bits and pieces.

The harmless sparrow's obliteration frightened me, in a way that the rooster fights didn't. A wave of fear churned into me, and my hands trembled.

Connie Knight

"Give me my gun, Henry," Gregory said. "Set it on the floor and I'll pick it up. We won't go looking for treasure until I get it back."

The idea of treasure made Henry cooperate. "Here's your Glock. My rifle's in my truck. I'll just get it later." He set the gun on the barn floor and walked away. Gregory walked over and picked it up.

Glock? Treasure? I moved over a little bit, so I could see into the room in the barn's corner. A shaft of sunlight streamed into the room, highlighting a spot next to the sleeping bag. In the center of the highlight sat a large briefcase, almost as big as a suitcase. I'd never seen it before, but I was willing to bet it was Professor Harrison's container for the camping shovel—the briefcase that had gone missing from the cemetery when Donny and Aunt Hettie ran away and before the police arrived.

I stood quietly where I was while Gregory coaxed his gun back from Henry. When that was done, Henry retreated into the room and slammed the door.

Glock, treasure, canping shovel. Gun shooting skills as good as Henry Hargrove's. What kind of project did Henry mean? And where were they going to look for treasure? Did Henry agree to help Gregory dig up something in the Hargrove Family Cemetery?

That seemed likely.

Gregory was standing between me and the barn door, still holding his Glock. I circled around him, so I could be closer to the door. My knees were shaking, my hands trembled, and I knew fear showed on my face. I avoided looking directly at Gregory Jackson, and tried to make my voice sound cheerful and sprightly.

"I don't want to interfere with your project, so I'll just mosey along," I said, edging toward the door and, in the distance, Janet's car.

Gregory looked at me. Mistrust had returned to his face. "Don't you need us to help you rescue Janet?"

"I need some help, but I can drive to Yorktown. You don't need to interrupt your plans." I edged a little more toward the door. I was afraid to say goodbye, turn around with my back to Gregory, and normally walk away.

"Oh, we don't mind helping," Gregory said. "Maybe you and Janet can help us with our project once we've rescued her."

I didn't want to know how we'd help with the project. "There's a map in the car; it shows the way to the place where Janet is stranded. I'll go get it right now."

"No, you won't," said Gregory flatly. "You seem to be upset about something. What is it?" The Glock gun was in his hand, pointing in my direction.

"I'm not upset," I lied, and then I took a deep breath and asked a question. He wasn't letting me go anyway. "Professor Harrison was shot by a Glock. Did you shoot him?"

Gregory snorted. "Oh, yes. Someone's figuring it out at last, and I don't mean Henry Hargrove."

"Why would you do that? You're in so much trouble at school without him."

"That'll smooth out eventually, but I'm better off without Harrison. That bastard! He made me do a lot of research about his family, far exceeding any relevance to my dissertation. Then, when I diagnosed the place where 'the treasure' was buried, that skunk went there without me! He would have dug everything up and kept it for himself."

"So you followed him to the cemetery and you shot him there."

"Yes. You're right. But now I can't let you go. You might tell someone, and I'll be arrested for murder. Henry hasn't figured it out; that's why he's part of my project."

Gregory lifted his head. "Henry!" he shouted. "Bring me that big briefcase. I need it now."

Henry lugged the briefcase out and laid it on the floor. "Open it," commanded Gregory, still waving his gun at me.

Henry opened the briefcase. It held another camping shovel like the one found in Harrison's hand, and a stack of documents,

Connie Knight

and some other things as well.

"Bring me the rope," Gregory said, and Henry obediently picked up the coil of white rope like clothesline. He held it out to Gregory.

Gregory didn't take it. "You'll have to do this. She wants to turn us in. She thinks our project is illegal, and disapproves of us. So take that rope and tie her hands behind her back, then tie her feet together."

Henry cheerfully followed the order. "We'll come back later on today and turn her loose, won't we?"

"Sure we will, but right now, she's coming with us. We'll put her in the back of your truck and she can help us with the project."

Henry drove the truck around front, and the two of them picked me up and slung me into the truck bed. I wrestled myself up into a sitting position, leaning against the cab.

Gregory and Henry closed up the barn. They put the big briefcase into the cab of the truck, and then climbed into it themselves. Off we drove.

My mind raced, thinking of things that might help me escape. There was the voice-mail I'd left for Bob Bennett, mentioning the old ranch house as a place where I'd try to find help for Janet. Janet's car, with my purse in it, could be seen from the road when someone passed the gap in the trees. Then there was my cell phone. It was in my jacket's pocket.

I'd have to figure out how to get to it, how to use it, when and where. Somehow.

CHAPTER FIFTEEN

Almost two hours had passed. Janet looked at her wristwatch every few minutes. It showed that time marched on even though nothing else changed. The javelina was still curled up in the roots of her oak tree, taking a nap. His cohorts had wandered off, probably not far away.

From her tree top, Janet had a good view of the surrounding land of grass and cactus. Looking down the road, or trail, in the direction where the historic cemetery was located—possibly—she saw a grove of large oak trees. It cut off any further view. Janet climbed a little higher in her tree, but still nothing like a cemetery appeared.

The third time she looked, there was something. A dark square speck came forward. It made slow progress, but became larger and more detailed as it approached. A car—no, an SUV—was bouncing down the remnants of the road. It would soon pass right by Janet's tree, veering in her tree's direction to avoid the huge pothole. The SUV must contain a person, or a party, who attended the cemetery dedication. Why else would they be driving through this neglected land?

Janet crawled out on a tree branch, the lowest and most likely from which she would be visible to the SUV driver. She wriggled out of her bright red jacket and held it out almost over the road. She flapped it back and forth. Surely it would get the driver's attention.

It did. The SUV continued down the road, swerved before reaching the pothole, and stopped under the oak tree. The javelina was now awake, and stood at the foot of the oak tree, snorting. The driver opened a roof window on the SUV, stood on the seat of his vehicle, and stuck his head and shoulders out of the sunroof.

He looked for the source of the waving red jacket. "Janet! What are you doing here?"

"Josh Gaines! I never thought I'd be so glad to see you. What are you doing here?"

"I tried to attend the dedication of the Owens cemetery. I must have made the wrong turn, though, because I never did find anything but more land like this."

"We did the same thing. Caroline and I followed a map, but we turned on this ranch road by mistake. When we stopped here, I got out of the car to look for tire tracks, and that wild hog chased me up into this tree." While they were talking, Josh moved over in the sunroof window and Janet carefully descended from the low tree branch to the top of the SUV. Josh extended a hand, and helped her crawl over to the roof window. He moved out of the way, and Janet clambered down from the roof top into the vehicle. The wild hog seemed to lose interest, and trotted away.

Janet slid down into the passenger's seat. "Oh, Josh, thank you! Caroline drove off in my car to get some help, and she should have been back here by now. We've got to find her. She must have got lost. Let's get to a place where the cell phones work so we can call her. She doesn't know these roads; that's why I've been driving us around."

"You can give me directions, please, when we reach the real road. The dirt roads and the ranch roads look alike to me."

The SUV bounced along, eventually reaching the unlocked ranch gate and the county dirt road. "Left or right?" Josh asked.

"Left. That will take us back to Yorktown, and I'm pretty sure that's the direction Caroline would have gone."

The dirt road was smooth and wide compared to the ranch road with potholes. Josh drove faster, but he and Janet each looked out on their side of the road, searching for Janet's car parked and stranded, or Caroline walking the rest of the way to Yorktown.

"I don't think my car would have run out of gas, or had a flat tire. Maybe there was an accident."

"Let's hope not."

They approached the ranch house up for sale and came to the gap in the trees. "Here are two cars," Josh said, slowing down. "Do you recognize them?"

"One of them is mine!" Janet cried. "She must be here. I don't recognize the other car, though, and I know the house is vacant. It's for sale. Maybe Caroline called someone and asked them to meet her here."

"Maybe." Josh eased the SUV up the dirt driveway leading to the ranch house, and parked it next to Janet's maroon sedan. The other car, gray in color, sat nearby.

Janet hopped out of the SUV. "Caroline!" she shouted, but there was no answer. The maroon sedan was empty, and the doors were unlocked. Car keys hung in the ignition, and the car started when Janet turned it on. Plenty of gas, no flat tire. Two purses were on the floor of the passenger side. One was Janet's and the other belonged to Caroline. Janet also noted a rusty chain and a padlock lying on the floor of her car. Where that came from, she didn't know.

Josh ambled over to Janet and the car. He saw the two purses. "Yours and Caroline's?"

Janet nodded.

"Maybe that means she's here somewhere. Let's look around."

Janet took both purses and the car keys then followed Josh to the ranch house. The doors were locked but they saw the empty rooms through the windows.

"Let's try the barn." Josh cautiously opened the barn door and they both peered inside.

Nobody was there, not even in the little room with a sleeping bag and an ice chest full of food.

"Caroline!" Janet called, but Josh said, "She's not here. That car with two purses in it worries me. She wouldn't have left them behind, would she?"

"No," Janet whispered. "Do you think she is in danger somehow? Normally I wouldn't think of that, but your relative was shot in our graveyard less than two weeks ago. Something is wrong here. Something different is going on."

"I think we should call the local police and notify them that she's missing. Let's give them the gray car's license plate number, too. Maybe that will help."

"I'll call Bob Bennett. The cell phones work from here." Janet retrieved her phone from her purse, and noticed that Caroline's phone was missing from its pocket on Caroline's purse. "Maybe she has it with her. I'll try calling her too."

"Call the cops first."

Janet dialed the number for Constable Bennett.

He answered, and listened intently to Janet's frantic account of the morning's activities and the disappearance of Caroline. "Do you want the license plate number of the car that's still here at the ranch house?"

Bob took the number. "I'll turn this in at the office; they can trace it. Right now I'm at your Uncle Cotton's house. You and Josh wait where you are. I'll be there as soon as I can."

Cotton was standing near Bob and had heard the conversation. "Need help?"

"I can use it. Your niece Caroline is missing."

Half an hour later, Bob's patrol car pulled up in the driveway of the vacant ranch house, followed by Uncle Cotton's truck with a gun in the rifle rack and a quartet of his best hound dogs riding in the truck bed. Janet saw them and came running forward, followed by Josh Gaines. Janet headed for Uncle Cotton, who opened his arms and gave her a hug. "We'll find her," he said. "She can't be gone very far."

Janet wiped her eyes with the handkerchief he offered. Uncle Cotton stepped to the back of the truck and let two of his dogs out.

154

"Do we have something for scent?"

Bob held up a green cardigan sweater he'd found in Janet's car. "This is Caroline's, isn't it, Janet?"

She nodded. "Yes. She left it in my car a couple of days ago."

Uncle Cotton took it and held it to the dogs. They sniffed it, found the scent, and followed it from the driveway into the small barn, then back to the driveway again. They couldn't find a scent to follow any further.

Bob's cell phone rang. His office called about the car whose license plate number he had reported. The car belonged to Gregory Jackson of San Antonio.

"Did any of you see Gregory Jackson here recently?" Bob asked. Cotton and Josh shook their heads, but Janet nodded hers.

"Oh, yes! We saw him and Uncle Henry Hargrove in a restaurant yesterday morning," Janet said, stuttering in excitement. "First they were arguing, and then they made friends. We heard they had dinner together last night. Maybe they were both here and drove off in Uncle Henry's truck."

"If they did that, where would they go?" Bob asked. "Any ideas?"

Josh answered, "It would probably be the Hargrove cemetery. My cousin Tom Harrison had a special interest in it, and Jackson worked with him on various historical projects. I don't know what might interest your Uncle Henry."

"Treasure," Janet said promptly. "I've heard him mention that more than once."

"What kind of treasure?"

"I don't know. Maybe there isn't any, but he seems to think there is."

Bob and Cotton discussed a plan while Cotton put his two hounds back into the truck bed.

"We're going to the cemetery. Maybe we'll find them there, or at least a scent trail," Bob finally said to Josh and Janet. "You two can follow us if you want, but be careful. Keep some distance while we're checking things out."

"Your car or mine?" Janet asked Josh.

"Mine," he said. "Better bring both purses along; don't leave anything in your car. Doesn't your cell phone work? Bring it along; we might be able to use it."

The caravan headed down the ranch's driveway: Bob in the patrol car, Uncle Cotton and the hounds in his pickup truck, then Josh and Janet in the SUV. "You'll have to give me directions, Janet. I don't know my way around here."

"I'll be the navigator," Janet said. "That's what Caroline says sometimes, when she has a map. I drive, and she tries to tell me where to go."

Josh laughed. "Is that what happened this morning?"

"No, the trouble was with the map in the invitation. We both misread it. Or maybe there was a mistake in the drawing."

"Maybe somebody copied the map in the cemetery book at the library. That's what I followed, and we ended up at the same pothole."

"Well, I'm grateful that we did. I'd still be stuck in the tree if you hadn't rescued me."

Josh smiled, pleased with Janet's gratitude.

He's a whole lot nicer now than at the funeral, Janet thought. *Please, Lord, let us find Caroline and make our way home, and I'll invite him to dinner tonight. We'll all go to Stockman's and celebrate surviving.*

* * *

Uncle Henry drove his pickup truck to the cemetery. Maybe he was still influenced by last night's alcohol, because he drove too fast. The truck bounced on the red dirt road, and I bounced around in the truck bed. With my hands tied behind my back, I had little control. I tried to loosen the ropes so I could wriggle out of them. No success. I couldn't reach the cell phone in my jacket pocket, either, and soon we would be out of the zone where it worked.

When we reached the cemetery, Henry pulled the truck up beside the chain-link fence. He didn't try to hide it. He and Gregory came to the truck bed where I lay. They let the tailgate down and pulled me up so I was sitting on it.

"Cut the ropes," Gregory said, and handed Henry a knife. Henry sliced the ropes without cutting me. My hands and feet were numb and I could barely stand up when they lifted me from the truck's tailgate and set me on the ground.

"Come along; walk," Gregory said. "You'll get back to normal in a few minutes." I could see the gun bulging in his corduroy jacket pocket. I tried to walk, and did better than I thought I could. The numbness of my hands diminished as we approached the grave of Thomas Watson Hargrove, and the patch of Cemetery Whites beside it.

Gregory had carried the large briefcase from the truck to the tombstone. He set it down, opened it, removed the collapsible shovel, and assembled it. Then he held it toward me. "Here you go," he said. "Let's see you find the treasure."

I took the shovel but protested, "I don't want to dig up this old grave."

Gregory pulled his gun out of his pocket. "You don't have to dig up the grave. Dig up the flower bed. That's where the treasure is hidden."

Uncle Henry must have been getting sober. "I'll do the work. You don't have to force it on her," he said.

Gregory snapped back at Henry, "I'm the boss, don't forget that. She can do the digging."

Henry subsided, and I started shoveling up the clumps of blooming irises, the Cemetery Whites. I'd reached the center of the flower bed before the shovel ran into something about a foot down.

Gregory heard the sound of the thump. "That's it! That's it!" He'd put his gun back in his pocket, but now he pulled it out again. "Keep on going. Let's dig that treasure chest out of the ground."

157

I shoveled more dirt away. A square shape appeared, and I shoveled away the dirt at its sides. It didn't take too long. The box was small, maybe two feet long, one foot wide, less than one foot deep. I pulled at it gently with my hands, and it came loose from its place in the soil, beneath the Cemetery Whites.

"Bring it here," rasped Gregory. Uncle Henry was almost as excited. I set the box on the ground, close to where they were standing. There were no tables or large tombstones around.

"Open it," Gregory said, pointing his gun at me. I tried, but the wooden box was hard to open. The wood was swollen, and the top wouldn't come loose from the bottom.

"Henry," Gregory snapped, nodding at the box. Henry came over with his knife and pried off the wooden lid.

The two men were eager to see the contents, but a metal box, almost as big as the wooden one, had to be extracted and opened. Then, there was a sheet of waterproof canvas wrapped around the contents.

Henry lifted the package with trembling hands. The fabric cracked, and out fell a number of documents—letters, a journal, perhaps invoices and deeds. So that was the treasure to Professor Harrison! I stood up to get out of Henry's way.

He threw the package down into the metal box. "Where's the treasure?" he shouted in anger. "Where's the diamonds and the gold?"

"I never said that was the treasure," Gregory sneered at Uncle Henry. "You just imagined it was. I can't help the way you think. I knew it would be historical treasure, because that's what Professor Harrison had me researching for. He wouldn't approve my dissertation without the extra work I did for him."

With a roar, Uncle Henry stood up from the iris patch and turned on Gregory like one gamecock on another. His fists were raised and his face was furious.

Gregory raised his Glock and pulled the trigger. The bullet hit Uncle Henry, and he fell back on the ground, almost in the same spot that had held Professor Harrison.

"Pick up the box," Gregory ordered, pointing the gun at me. My hands were trembling, but I picked it up as quickly as I could. I collected the letters and things that had fallen on the ground and put them in the metal box, too.

"What will we do about my Uncle Henry? He's stopped breathing."

"So he has. Too bad." Gregory picked up the shovel, took a handkerchief out of a pocket, and wiped the shovel's handle to erase fingerprints. He then placed the shovel in Henry's hand. He kept a close eye on me while he did these things. If I had thought of a practical escape, I'd have been afraid to try it.

"We'll leave him and his truck here. It'll look like he did the digging. We'll cut into the woods and head back to the barn. I'll get my car from there."

We started walking. Gregory carried the document box and I carried the briefcase. I had to walk in front, following Gregory's directions about which way to go. I knew he was holding his gun on me, and I knew he'd use it on me eventually. He'd shot Tom Harrison and Henry Hargrove already. If he could get me out of the way, maybe there would be no witnesses. Maybe he could slide back into his normal life, resume his studies and his teaching assistantship. He could wait a while, and invent another place for having found his treasure of historical documents.

We walked and walked. At least an hour passed. I was pretty sure we were back in a cell phone zone, but there was no benefit from it. With Gregory right behind me, I couldn't make a phone call. I didn't even dare to touch the phone in my jacket pocket; Gregory would see it and take the phone away.

I thought of Janet. I hoped someone had found her by now. It was mid-afternoon, and nobody would miss Janet or me until suppertime. Janet might sit in her tree until midnight, unless someone from the cemetery dedication happened to pass by.

Meanwhile, I walked on, thankful I'd worn leather flats instead of high heels when dressing for the cemetery dedication. I tried to think of some way to prevent Gregory from shooting me, but so far nothing came into my mind.

* * *

Constable Bennett, Cotton and the hounds, and Josh and Janet pulled up and parked their vehicles by the chain-link fence of the Hargrove Family Cemetery. They parked in line behind a red pickup truck, which was next to the fence's open gate.

"That's Uncle Henry's truck," Janet told Bob when the four of them assembled by the open gate. "If he's here, Gregory Jackson might be with him."

"Caroline might be with them, too," Bob said grimly. "Stay here." He pulled his gun from its holster. With it, and followed by Cotton Hargrove with his rifle and his hounds, Bob walked into the cemetery. He headed toward the probable place of finding someone: the grave of Thomas Watson Hargrove and the patch of Cemetery Whites.

They cautiously edged around the few trees and groves of bushes, following the path to the oldest part of the cemetery. Scrub brush and trees grew outside the cemetery's chain-link fence. Bob and Cotton were wary of someone hiding there and aiming at them with a pistol.

Cotton's hounds were whining. They had picked up Caroline's scent. They led the way to the iris patch; Bob and Cotton followed. They skirted a stand of small trees, guns ready, to confront anyone at the grave site.

The man they found was lying on the ground. There was a shovel in his hand, and a dark red spot on the front of his shirt.

"Henry Hargrove," Bob whispered. The sight sickened him: same setting, different man. "I'll call the ambulance. They're nearby and know the way here."

Cotton nodded. "I'm going to set my hounds loose. They've

picked up Caroline's scent. She must have escaped from here on foot, or maybe Jackson is with her."

"They're probably heading back to the barn where Jackson's car is parked. I'll call my office and the ambulance. Soon as someone gets here, I'll drive to the barn and search for them from there. Got your cell phone?"

"Yep."

"It works near the ranch house. I'll call you if I find them."

"Same here. I'll call you too." They cued their cell phones to vibrate instead of ring—silence could be important—and Cotton loosed his hounds. They ran off, barking, and Cotton loped behind them, an old man still in excellent shape.

Janet and Josh had walked to the gravesite and saw Uncle Henry lying on the ground. Janet knelt down next to him and took his hand in hers. "Oh, Uncle Henry, what kind of treasure were you looking for! Nothing could be worth this."

Then she dropped his hand and screamed. "He squeezed my hand! He must be alive. His hand is warm, too." She felt his wrist for a pulse and found one. "Bob! What can we do?"

"I've already called the ambulance. Just sit tight. They'll be here soon."

Josh walked over to the iris patch where Uncle Henry lay. He saw the square hole that the wooden box had occupied. He saw the box, in two pieces, lying nearby. Obviously it had been torn apart and discarded.

"They found something," he observed. "Can't be too heavy. I'd say it's not bars of gold."

Uncle Henry moaned. "Letters," he whispered, and then slipped back into unconsciousness.

The ambulance arrived, speeding down the dirt road and screeching to a halt. Uncle Henry was soon on a stretcher, placed in the ambulance with a technician who got him started on an IV and emergency medications.

"We're taking him to St. Joseph's. It's got a good emergency room. From there, he may be transferred to the hospital in Victoria." The ambulance turned around and sped off.

"He may live while my cousin died," Josh blurted. His gold-rimmed glasses glinted in the sunlight.

"Your cousin got hit from a longer distance, but the bullet went into his heart. He died instantly," Bob told him gently. "If we had found him earlier, we still couldn't have saved him. You might miss him, but things couldn't have been any different."

Josh blinked back his tears and nodded. "Some things are under control, and some are just random. Do the best you can; that's what I think."

"Good thinking. Let's go back to the barn. You can follow me in the SUV, but stay on the road. Don't drive into the ranch; it could be dangerous if Gregory Jackson has returned there. My partner will meet me there. You two take care of yourselves and stay where it's safe."

* * *

We walked on and on. I thought we were approaching the ranch house; I saw glimpses of it as we made our way through the brush. So did Gregory. He still walked behind me with the gun at my back, but I could tell the view of the house took his attention. His directions were less frequent and sometimes he changed his mind. He was distracted by approaching the house. How to get to his car and drive away without becoming visible to anyone passing by, that's what occupied his mind now.

At the ranch, the cell phones worked. If only I could get mine out of my pocket! I could punch just a couple of buttons to call Bob Bennett. Maybe I could say something to Gregory that Bob would overhear on the phone; then he would come rescue me. I could say, *Gregory, isn't that the vacant ranch house not too far ahead?* and Bob would overhear it and know where I was.

But did he know about the trouble I was in? Only if Janet had been rescued, and looked for me, and called Bob to say I was missing, could anyone have given my absence a thought. Janet and I were supposed to be gone all day, driving to the Owens cemetery dedication and back, attending the reception at someone's house, maybe going to a historical museum. Who'd miss us?

Gregory interrupted my thoughts. "Keep going toward the house," he commanded. "Once there, we'll run for my car and drive away." But something distracted him as he was speaking, and I heard it too.

It was the baying of the hounds, confident of the path they were running. They must be Uncle Cotton's hounds! They must be following our scents.

"Let's keep moving," Gregory said. "We need to get to the car and drive away before they see us. They won't know I shot Henry if we get out of here fast enough."

You're grabbing at straws, I thought, but didn't tell him. *If Uncle Cotton was tracking us down, he must have started at the cemetery. Bob Bennett would have been contacted, and Janet must have been involved. Somehow she got out of the tree.*

I walked faster, but the hounds were getting closer. Why should I drive away with you? I thought. *I'm a witness to your shooting Uncle Henry. You know that and you'll shoot me eventually.*

The hounds bayed louder, and Uncle Cotton called my name. "Caroline! Where are you?"

Gregory stepped forward and clamped his hand over my mouth. "Don't answer him!" He poked his gun into my back. "Keep going. Let's get to that car ASAP."

I walked faster and faster with Gregory right behind me. Then I tripped over something hidden by the grass, and I fell to the ground. I landed on my hands and knees, but somehow my ankle was twisted.

"Gregory, I can't stand up," I told him, exaggerating the truth somewhat. "Go on without me. You can run faster, get to the car, and drive away."

Connie Knight

He raised his gun and pointed it at me, but there was hesitancy in his face.

"If you shoot me, they'll know it was you," I told him. "You're better off just running to escape." I saw the hounds behind him, running through the grass, getting closer to us every second.

They bayed and he heard them, and then turned around to face Uncle Cotton. He couldn't see me. I grabbed him by his ankles and gave them a good hard jerk. He fell to the ground and the gun flew out of his hand. I picked it up and pointed it at him. He was still on the ground, somewhat stunned by the sudden fall.

"Don't move," I said. "If I have to shoot you, I will."

Uncle Cotton ran up, carrying his rifle. He saw that I held the gun, not Jackson, and he pointed his rifle at the man on the ground.

"I'll guard him. Call Bob and tell him where we are."

So at last I took the cell phone out of my pocket and called Bob. "Just listen for the hounds; that's where we are," I told him. "And please make sure you have the handcuffs. I'll feel a lot better when Gregory Jackson is in jail."

* * *

When I called him, Constable Bennett and his partner were near the ranch house in their patrol car. They drove up the driveway in a few minutes, arrested Gregory Jackson, and drove off with him in handcuffs, headed for the county jail.

When the constables left, Janet and Josh drove up the driveway and parked near where Uncle Cotton and I were still standing.

"What happened?" Janet demanded. I told her the story of my afternoon with Gregory Jackson and Uncle Henry, who was shot because he didn't like the treasure. "He died over it," I said. "Just like Professor Harrison."

"Oh, no! He survived." Janet told me her story about being rescued from the oak tree, driving to the ranch house with Josh, and calling Bob Bennett for help. Bob was with Uncle Cotton, who followed Bob to the ranch, and brought four hounds along to use if they were needed.

"They were needed. We all met here and did a search, but it didn't go anywhere. Josh suggested going to the cemetery, and we did. We found Uncle Henry, and I thought he was dead, but he still had a pulse, and the ambulance Bob called took him away. Uncle Cotton's hounds picked up your scent and followed your trail, and Uncle Cotton went with them, carrying his rifle. You know the rest of it. By the way, you remember Josh, don't you? We met him at the professor's funeral on Monday. Don't you remember him? He's Estelle Shawn's cousin."

I did, in a much different way than he currently deserved. Things must have changed. I put my hand out to shake his, and realized I was clutching the metal treasure box Gregory had dropped on the ground. I'd picked it up along with Gregory's gun.

Uncle Cotton and Josh had both listened to Janet and me. "I'd better load up the hounds and go home," Uncle Cotton said."The wolf hunt starts in a couple of hours, and I don't want my friends to miss me."

I couldn't believe what he said. "Didn't you already wear yourself out this afternoon?"

His face crinkled with a smile. "Oh, no. Did you?"

I stepped forward and gave him a big hug with one arm, still clutching the metal box with the other. He blushed but grinned. "You gonna keep that metal box of treasure, Caroline?" he asked.

"Can I?"

"Henry said there were letters in it. Can you read those letters, and the other ones too, and make a report for our next family meeting?"

"Uncle Cotton, that's a wonderful idea. Thanks for suggesting it. I'll take good care of this treasure."

He was loading his hounds into the truck as we spoke. "I look forward to hearing your report. Do you want to come to the wolf hunt?"

Connie Knight

Janet chimed in, "No, thanks anyway, Uncle Cotton. We're going to have dinner at Stockman Restaurant early this evening. I want to introduce Josh to my husband and my son Kenny. Bob Bennett is joining us, too."

"Well, I'll see you in church on Sunday." Uncle Cotton climbed into his truck, waved goodbye, and took off. The hounds barked goodbye.

"We've got to go home and change our clothes," I said to Janet. The wild hog never returned her shoes; she was walking around barefoot. My clothes were grubby from bouncing around in the back of Uncle Henry's pickup truck.

"We can do that and meet for dinner at six-thirty?"

"I suppose. How about if I ride with Josh and you lead us out of here? I don't want to risk getting lost. Josh, do you want to come home with me? I'll freshen up, then drive us over to Stockman's."

"Sounds fine."

"All right then." We got into our cars and headed on down the driveway, then down the road to Yorktown.

Cemetery Whites

CHAPTER SIXTEEN

While Josh drove me home, I held the metal box of papers in my lap, but I didn't open the box to look at the letters. I wanted to reserve them for special attention tomorrow, when I'd have plenty of time and energy to collate them with the documents from Miranda and Estelle.

Once home, I put the box away in a file cabinet drawer that locked. Then I made a pot of coffee, served some to Josh, and excused myself for a quick shower and a change of clothes. Josh still looked well-dressed and sparkling clean; he hadn't run from javelinas like Janet, or bounced on the bed of a pickup truck like me.

Freshly showered and dressed in clean clothes, I stepped out into the living room where Josh was watching TV. I poured us each a cup of coffee. We had another half-hour before driving to the Stockman Restaurant.

"Tell me a little about yourself, Josh," I said. "What brought you out here today? Whatever the reason, we're lucky you appeared where you did, in time to help Janet and me."

Josh set his cup down. "No important reason. After talking with you at the funeral, I went home and looked DeWitt County things up on the computer. I found out about the Owens cemetery restoration and the dedication this morning, so I decided to attend. I've become interested in local Texas history, I guess. It's more interesting than it used to be."

"I know just what you mean. That's how I got into all this research myself." I took our empty cups and put them in the kitchen sink. "Ready for dinner? I'll drive; you take a break. Stockman's is just a few blocks from here."

"Sure. That will be nice."

We left the house and I drove us to the restaurant.

Jordan and Janet were already seated at a large round table at the end of the room. Josh and I joined them, and Janet introduced Josh to her husband as "the man who rescued me before you'd have to".

"Thanks for saving me from hours of worry," Jordan said, shaking hands with Josh. "It's a real blessing that you got lost in the same place as Caroline and Janet. Next time you come here, call me. I'll be glad to show you around." He gave Josh a business card, and Josh gave him one in return.

Bob Bennett joined us in a few more minutes. He'd just finished his day of work, which ended with driving to Cuero to book Gregory Jackson, question him, and fill out the necessary paperwork. He looked tired, and ordered coffee when the waitress came to our table. I knew he wanted to restore his energy, and I hoped the coffee would help.

Maury and Elizabeth were helping Uncle Cotton host the wolf hunt, so I didn't expect them to join us. To my surprise, Allen Boyce and Martha McNair walked into the restaurant in a few more minutes. Janet waved them over to our table.

"How nice to see you! Won't you join us? We have lots of news to share. Oh, let me introduce Josh Gaines to you. Josh, these are Martha McNair and Allen Boyce, an engaged couple interested in buying the ranch house we visited this afternoon."

Allen, Martha and Josh shook hands, and then Martha exclaimed, "We have some news, too! We made an offer on the ranch house yesterday, and it has been accepted. I'm thrilled with Allen's plans for renovation, and I can't wait to get started. And, before we close on the house, we're going to get married!"

She glowed, and Allen beamed, as she related their news and they found seats at the table. "So what's your news?' she asked.

Cemetery Whites

"It involves your house, but not in a happy way." Janet, Josh, and I told Martha and Allen our story, and Bob wrapped it up with the details of putting Gregory Jackson in jail.

"I went by the hospital to check on Henry Hargrove," he added. "His condition is stable, but he'll be in the hospital for a few days. Maybe we can visit him tomorrow, Caroline. He was asking about you."

"Okay," I said. We'd work it out later. Right now, the waitress was taking orders, and the focus of conversation shifted, centering on Josh's interest in history, Allen's renovation plans, and Martha's plans for the wedding. Janet asked Martha about Lisa's band and the Western music performance at the library next week.

By the time dinner ended, I was totally tuckered out. I drove home, returning Josh to his SUV, and Bob followed us. He parked his car and walked me to the door of my cottage after we said goodbye to Josh.

"I think Jackson is the only danger to us, and he's in jail, but just in case someone else is interested in that treasure chest of letters, I'd like to stay with you tonight. I'll sleep on the sofa, but I want to make sure you're safe."

"You don't have to sleep on the sofa," I said. I unlocked the front door, and we walked into the living room together.

* * *

I slept late Friday morning. Bob woke up earlier, made himself some coffee and breakfast, answered phone calls and took messages for me. When I woke up, it was almost noon. Bob found a tray in the kitchen and brought some coffee and breakfast to me.

He delivered the phone messages he'd jotted down while I was still asleep. Estelle Shawn called; her cousin Josh Gaines had told her all about the events of yesterday. Maury and Elizabeth called; they'd heard the news from Uncle Cotton. Donny and Aunt Hettie called; they'd visited Uncle Henry, still in the small local hospital.

He'd actually expressed concern about me! Donny and Aunt Hettie wanted to be sure I was all right; so did Danny and Uncle Darryl Harrell.

Bob had taken the day off; his office called him on his cell phone to let him know that Gregory Jackson had been charged with murder regarding Professor Harrison, and attempted murder regarding Henry Hargrove. His Glock gun's bullets matched the one that killed Professor Harrison. They wanted to interview me about the shooting of Henry Hargrove, and about my being kidnapped, but tomorrow would do. Bob told them I needed some rest.

After breakfast, I took a shower and dressed in comfortable jeans and a tee shirt. I wanted to stay at home, lounge around, and take a look at the letters in the metal box.

"Do you mind?" I asked Bob. "You can look at them with me if you want to."

Bob grinned. "I don't mind. I'll find something to watch on TV. Maybe I'll take a nap. Wake me up if you need something."

He kissed me and went to the sofa in the living room, and I went into my study.

* * *

I created three stacks of documents on my trestle table: Miranda's, Estelle's, and the metal box, along with the stack I'd started. It consisted of letters collated by date. Then I opened the metal box.

There were letters from Caroline Jane, Sarah Elizabeth, Priscilla, and Willie, all of them writing to all of each other. Caroline Jane's journal was in good shape; the pages were not stuck to each other, and the ink had not faded away. Then there were the legal documents: a map, a deed, and a will. And something in an envelope, addressed to "The Hargrove Family".

I spent more than an hour organizing the letters by date. I couldn't help stopping to read a passage in one letter or another now and then.

Then I assembled documents summarizing portions of the past. First came cousin Miranda's account of Caroline Jane's childhood during the Civil War, when she and Willie both used rifles to hunt for game and to defend the household against Indian raids. They worked together looking after the farm, and both were educated by Sarah and Priscilla. After the Civil War, when Caroline Jane married James Jamison and moved to his isolated ranch, Willie went with her. Her husband rode on vigilante raids with the Sutton side of the vicious feud, and Willie helped develop the ranch. He became the ranch foreman/manager.

Then the metal box letters and Caroline Jane's journal began to come forth with new information. As Miranda wrote, James Jamison resented his wife's independence and became verbally abusive, physically abusive, too.

In her journal, Caroline Jane wrote about her source of friendship and comfort on the ranch. She'd go to Willie, cry on his shoulder, and listen to his advice. During one of James' vigilante trips, the friendship with Willie turned into romance. Their love for each other, long existing, was finally acknowledged. Love kindled passion, and they spent every night of James' absence together in Willie's cabin.

Along with passion came fear. Racial hatred escalated and grew into violence during Reconstruction. Willie's love for Caroline Jane endangered his life if anyone found out—especially James Jamison.

Her husband came home briefly and left again several times over the next few months, and Caroline managed to keep her romance secret. Then that became impossible. She realized she was carrying a child, and the father must be Willie.

That's why she decided to return to the Hargrove homestead and ask her mother for help. First, she persuaded Willie to move to San Antonio. She didn't tell him why. She said she wanted to leave her husband, and gave Willie the name of a pastor in San Antonio, and the name of an integrated neighborhood—Ellis Alley, on the

East Side of town.

Willie traveled to San Antonio, called on the pastor, and became a teacher at the church's school. He found a house in Ellis Alley. His life quickly took a good, new shape, but he missed ranch life, missed Caroline Jane. He became a deacon of his church. He and Caroline Jane were out of touch. He wrote letters to Priscilla, his mother.

Caroline Jane arrived at last at the Oak Creek Hargrove homestead and told her family she was leaving her husband. He was negligent and abusive. Then, when he returned to his ranch, Jamison found her gone. He knew she went to her homestead. He sent word he would come after her and take her home, whether she wanted to go or not.

Then I looked at the document from the newspaper about the Sutton-Taylor Feud. It discussed the trip James Jamison made to Oak Creek, how Caroline Jane's father and brothers had barricaded the road to their house so they could talk with James and send him back home. How the sound of a shot came forth, James Jamison was found dead, and was buried at the bottom of the new grave they'd dug for Thomas Watson Hargrove, who was dying. Jamison's death and burial was a secret for generations—known to a certain extent but not acknowledged.

Finally, there were the notes I'd made after talking with Aunt Hettie. Caroline Jane was the one who shot her husband. He'd pulled a gun on her, and she was prepared. She shot him with her Henry rifle, and her brothers and father knew this but kept it secret. They'd heard the shot, galloped up the road, and found Caroline Jane with her rifle and her dead husband.

In spite of the secret burial and Thomas Watson Hargrove's funeral in the next few days, Caroline Jane's mother came up with a plan. Her son Tom would soon leave Texas for Arizona. Young, spirited, and adventuresome, he was planning to establish a ranch farther West. He was making plans to leave San Antonio with a wagon train in just a few weeks. His mother took him into her confidence and asked for his help. She'd send Priscilla along to take care of Caroline Jane, she said.

So Caroline Jane and Priscilla joined Tom on the day he traveled to San Antonio to join the wagon train leaving from there. He bought a wagon, oxen, horses, and all the equipment. Caroline Jane brought her rifle; Priscilla brought her Bible. She had agreed to travel with Caroline Jane out of love for her and her son Willie, and love for the baby to be born, who would be her grandchild.

The wagon train traveled across Texas plains to El Paso, then connected with the Gila Trail and eventually reached Tucson, Arizona. Caroline Jane and Priscilla found lodgings where they could stay for the winter. Tom rode off but would return; he wanted to see the ranch land for sale, to gather information about the area.

All of this was discussed in letters written back and forth during the wagon train trip, and during the months of winter in Tucson.

Caroline Jane's baby was born in Tucson in October. He was beautiful and healthy; he looked like Willie; he was robust and he thrived. This was written in letters to Sarah—secret letters that were hidden.

Eventually Priscilla had to tell Sarah that Caroline Jane was ill. She was tired, feverish, fading away. She was dying, and she knew it. She and Priscilla worked out a plan for raising the newly born boy, Josiah Gaines, named for his grandfather, Priscilla's husband, who died on the way from Mississippi to Texas. The two of them made a plan and called a lawyer to help write Caroline Jane's will.

Caroline Jane passed away and was buried in Tucson. Priscilla, Josiah, and Tom, when he returned, stayed through the winter in Tucson. In April, almost a year from the time they left San Antonio, Priscilla, with the baby, climbed into a stagecoach and started traveling back to San Antonio. Tom wished them goodbye. When they left, he rode off to his new ranch to build a house and establish a herd of cattle there.

Through letters, Sarah Hargrove and Willie Gaines both expected the arrival of Priscilla and baby Josiah Gaines. They waited one morning for the stagecoach to arrive, and around noon, it did. All three of them cried tears of joy in welcoming each other. Sarah accompanied the others to Willie's house in Ellis Alley. It was small, pretty, and clean, with two bedrooms and an extra room in the back that could be made into Josiah's room, when he was older.

They reviewed Caroline Jane's plan. Willie and Priscilla would raise Josiah, but he would be presented as an orphan that Priscilla had adopted in New Mexico. True parentage was a secret now; it could be acknowledged in the future, when public knowledge would not be so dangerous as it could be then. Sarah Hargrove, Josiah's grandmother, would see him from time to time and help finance his upbringing.

Then they looked at Caroline Jane's will. She left the Jamison ranch to her parents, with a section of five hundred acres left to Willie Gaines.

* * *

After that, the letters and documents ended. I picked up the Gaines family history booklet and read the biography of Josiah Gaines. He attended St. Peter Claver school for black children in San Antonio in its earliest days, and then St. Philip's College. He set up a grocery store in Ellis Alley. It succeeded, and he followed it with several other stores in other locations on the East Side. He married, had several children, and became the founder of a large and prosperous family, prominent in the black community from then until today.

There was one thing left to read: Priscilla's unopened letter.

To Whomever Opens This Letter, it began.

She had collected letters concerning the love of Caroline Jane and Willie, and their parentage of the child Josiah, her letter said. It wasn't time yet to acknowledge the couple's fate, but when that time came, these letters would be records of the Hargrove and Gaines family history. Priscilla buried the wooden chest with the metal box inside, and planted the Cemetery Whites iris bulbs on top as a

Cemetery Whites

marker. Her son Willie and her dear friend Sarah Hargrove knew about the buried chest. She trusted them to pass the information on to someone in the next generation, someone who would take the responsibility of retrieving the letters and would read them to learn the entire truth.

I put the letter down on the trestle table and glanced at the clock. Almost three-thirty on March 25, 2010, and someone had read Priscilla's letter at last. Why me? Why hadn't anybody found out about the chest earlier? Who had heard the secret from Willie or Sarah Hargrove, but hadn't passed it on?

Gregory Jackson might have found a clue that led Professor Harrison to the patch of Cemetery Whites. Maybe I could talk to him later, but for now—Friday afternoon—there was another source of information to pursue.

"Bob, how's the ball game going?" I asked. "Do you want to go to Cuero with me?"

He did, and he drove us there in his car. It didn't take long, and Bob knew where land records were held.

In the county buildings, there was a large room filled with tall, fat books bound in red vinyl, and older volumes hand-written and bound in leather. A clerk helped us look up the Jamison ranch and track its progress. In 1877, because of Caroline Jane's will, the ranch passed on to her parents, but the five hundred acres left to Willie was not processed. It was in probate.

In 1903, John David and Sarah Hargrove, elderly as they were, sold the ranch, but Willie's land was still in probate. The ranch sold twice again, most recently in the 1950s, and the five hundred acres still remained in probate.

"The ranchers probably use it and pay taxes on it," the clerk commented. "It's the corner area of the five thousand acre ranch. See this survey? The corner section is marked at twenty by twenty-five acres. That's probably the section that is still under probate after all these years."

We thanked the clerk and copied the documents, finishing just

175

Connie Knight

as the clock struck five and the office was closed.

Driving home, Bob finally asked, "What are you going to do about this?"

"I don't know. Talk to attorneys, I guess. Estelle Shawn and David Hargrove, for starts. Find out about the current ranch owner. I'm not sure anything can be done about the probate, especially on good terms. I just want to see how it could work."

"I wonder why it's still in probate."

"So do I. We may not find out, though. Not all secrets become revealed."

After dinner, I called Estelle Shawn, David Hargrove, and Janet, and told them what I had found—the secrets revealed and the will. We agreed on a meeting in San Antonio Saturday afternoon, and a family meeting at Uncle Cotton's on Wednesday. Josh would join Estelle at the meeting Saturday, and both were invited to the family meeting on Wednesday.

I invited Bob to the family meeting on Wednesday, and he accepted.

"Don't forget about Lisa's band at the library on Monday afternoon," Janet reminded me. "And don't you want to visit Great-Aunt Hettie and Uncle Henry? They might know something about that five hundred acres, or something about the owner of the ranch."

I agreed with Janet, and then I agreed with Bob. I might be busy on the other days, but we'd spend Saturday night and Sunday at his ranch, with time to ourselves and no intrusions.

Cemetery Whites

CHAPTER SEVENTEEN
Evening of Wednesday, March 31, 2010

At five-thirty on Wednesday evening, we'd meet at Stockman's for an early dinner, then we'd drive out to Uncle Cotton's house for the family meeting at seven o'clock. Estelle and Josh would leave their car at the restaurant and ride with Janet and Jordan; I'd ride with Bob.

I brought along two stacks of newspapers to make available at the meeting: last week's, with my first column, as an introduction; and today's, with a column reviewing Lisa's band's performance Monday afternoon at the library. The band's cowboy songs enchanted the school children, and Lisa taught them some songs to sing along at the end of each set. I wrote a glowing review and hoped the band would perform for the students annually.

I also brought a few copies of the Sunday Yorktown *Chronicle* with a headline about the arrest of Gregory Jackson. Television had also carried that story, and probably everyone attending the meeting had already heard that much of the news.

Finally, I brought the speech I'd written, based on the results of the research Janet and I had done, and the results of the Saturday meeting in San Antonio.

I felt nervous about making the speech and kept quiet through dinner. Janet and Estelle chatted vivaciously, with occasional comments from Josh, Jordan, and Bob. I listened, but didn't say much. In an hour, we left the restaurant and headed for Uncle Cotton's house.

When we arrived, the parking lot was almost full, even more

packed than last time. I saw a couple of motorcycles as well as Aunt Hettie's Oldsmobile and Uncle Henry's old pickup truck. He'd been released from the hospital yesterday to stay with Uncle Cotton for a few days. For various legal reasons, he wasn't charged with anything, mostly because he had told the police a lot about Jackson that would help them convict him. He had been very drunk while assisting Jackson with kidnapping me, and hadn't really understood what they were doing, so I forgave him somewhat, though not completely.

When we entered Uncle Cotton's back porch meeting room, I could see Uncle Henry sitting with Aunt Hettie and the twins—a good place to take cover. I wouldn't admonish him in front of them. Like Uncle Cotton, they valued him as family, forgave him, and wanted to help him improve his behavior. Lots of luck, I thought. I wasn't quite as optimistic as they were.

As we walked into the room, it was clear that more people than last time attended. A loud surge of conversation and laughter enveloped us. We hung up our jackets; Bob found a table to hold the stacks of newspapers he'd carried in; I made sure I had my written speech in my purse. Janet took Estelle and Josh through the room, introducing them by name only. She wasn't revealing any family secret relationships yet; she was leaving that to me.

I heard someone telling the Davy Crockett joke. "You never heard of Davy Crockett? Well, just go ahead and pull that trigger, you dumb ass son of a bitch." The group listening to the joke laughed as if they'd never heard it before, and the woman who told it happily accepted their applause.

David the lawyer saw me across the room and came over. "It's almost time to call the meeting. Come with me, and let's get Estelle and Josh, too." We left Bob behind and headed for the spot David used as a platform for speech. Janet, Josh, and Estelle stood nearby, and David beckoned them over.

Then he tapped a spoon on a glass to gain everyone's attention. "Okay if I preside?" he asked, just like last time.

No one objected. David introduced Estelle and Josh as descendants of Priscilla Gaines who had accompanied Sarah Gaines to Texas from Mississippi when she married John David Hargrove. "Something from the past that had faded away," he said. "Not a family secret, but something forgotten." He introduced Janet and me as "amateur detectives who took on the role of researching the murder of Professor Thomas Harrison. They discovered a great deal of material, and Caroline will tell you all about it in her speech."

The room fell quiet when I stepped forward, carrying my written speech in my hands.

"Good evening," I said. "If you read the Sunday Yorktown *Chronicle*, or watched the TV news, you already know a lot about who shot Professor Thomas Harrison. Gregory Jackson shot him. Jackson was a young man working on his doctorate in Texas history under the guidance of Professor Harrison, who manipulated him into researching the Gaines family history. The Harrisons are a recent branch of the Gaineses. The professor believed that Priscilla Gaines had buried some family treasure, but he didn't know what or where. Gregory Jackson stumbled across a clue and told the professor about it, but Harrison excluded him from digging up the treasure and sharing it. In anger, Jackson followed Harrison to our family cemetery, where the professor started digging up the treasure. Gregory Jackson, hidden in the underbrush outside the cemetery fence, shot the professor down and left him dead. He also left the treasure behind, intending to dig it up later.

"As it turned out, I was the one who found the treasure. I was kidnapped and forced to dig it up myself. It wasn't diamond jewelry, or bars of gold. It was a wooden chest containing a metal box filled with letters, a journal, and a will.

"Gregory Jackson and Uncle Henry began arguing over the treasure, and Jackson shot Uncle Henry. Then he took off with me at gunpoint, running to escape capture and arrest. Fortunately, thanks to the actions of Janet Jordan and Josh Gaines, Bob Bennett and his partner, and Uncle Cotton with his hounds who chased us

Connie Knight

down, Uncle Henry and I were both rescued. Uncle Henry got the ambulance to take him to the emergency clinic, and I got custody of the treasure box to take home with me.

"I'd already accumulated family records, starting with those from cousin Miranda, and followed by letters and a booklet of the Gaines family history from Estelle Shawn. Janet and I attended the funeral of Estelle's brother, Thomas Harrison, and were surprised to find out that their family is descended from an orphan child, named Josiah Gaines, who was raised by Priscilla Gaines and her son Willie —former slaves of John David and Sarah Hargrove, whose maiden name was Gaines. Her family sent Priscilla and Willie to Texas with Sarah when she married John David Hargrove, but they retained the name Gaines. They both eventually moved to San Antonio after the Civil War, after they became free.

"A statement from Aunt Hettie answered another question. We knew the story of Caroline Jane Jamison running away from her abusive husband, who followed her to her homestead. He was shot and buried—the second corpse in Thomas Watson Hargrove's grave. But when I asked Aunt Hettie who did the shooting, she knew! Caroline Jane Jamison lay in wait for her husband farther up the road from her father and brothers. She called her husband's name, he pulled out his gun, and she shot him.

"So how many secrets have we uncovered already? There are more to come. I'd been organizing the letters obtained from Miranda and Estelle by date, but somehow there were no letters from Caroline Jane. These were found in the treasure chest that Priscilla put together and buried.

"The secret they uncover is about the long-term friendship between Caroline Jane and Willie, who grew up together and established the Jamison ranch together. Friendship eventually turned into love, and love turned into pregnancy. Caroline Jane feared her husband's behavior if he found out. He could deny the existence of love, claim it was rape, and gather his vigilante group to lynch Willie. Then what would happen to the child when it was born? Caroline Jane didn't tell Willie about the child she carried. She told him she was leaving the ranch and going home. She persuaded Willie to move to San Antonio, to Ellis Alley. She gave him the name of a church pastor to contact, and Willie found a job and a house in San Antonio.

"Even after her husband's death, Caroline Jane couldn't return to the ranch. Because she was pregnant, she traveled West with her brother Tom who was moving there. Priscilla accompanied her. They arrived in Tucson just before the baby was born, but Caroline Jane didn't survive. She became frail, faded away, and died.

"So Priscilla returned to San Antonio with the baby—Willie's son, not an orphan—and the large, prosperous Gaines family had its founder. The real founding parents were Willie and Caroline Jane, but their parentage was kept secret. Josiah Gaines was presented as an orphan, and the relationship of the Gaines family as a branch of the Hargrove family was known to a very few who died long ago.

"Priscilla Gaines and Sarah Hargrove stayed in touch, and Sarah sometimes visited her grandson and helped provide for his education and for establishing his first store.

"So there's one secret left. What was in the will I found in the treasure box? Caroline Jane wrote the will in Tucson. She left the Jamison ranch to her parents, with a five-hundred-acre section left to Willie Gaines. But Willie never claimed it. Today, more than a century later, it's still in probate.

"What to do? Can the Gaines family make a claim for the land at this time? Would they want to?

"Well, we've started working on that. David and Estelle, both lawyers, met on Saturday afternoon to discuss the legal issues of the probate. Josh, Janet, and I attended the meeting. Yesterday, all of us met with the owner of the ranch—a very nice elderly woman who has plans for the future of her ranch. She's leaving it to the State of Texas as a park, and she's willing to cede her claim to the five hundred acres if the Gaines family would include it as part of the park. They would still have the right to build some houses and roads, and use the land for housing or camping. That's something to be worked out, and Estelle is taking it on as a special project.

"So that's the end of my speech. I'll be glad to answer any questions, but let's do that by e-mail. Right now, I've talked about all I can for one evening."

The family remained silent as I stepped away from my place of speech. They were stunned by the information I'd revealed—the solutions to two murders, and the family secrets. Finally, someone began to applaud, and the rest of the crowd joined in. I felt a wave of relief. I'd had some fear of being admonished for revealing all those secrets.

The Gaines family was now acknowledged as a branch of the Hargrove clan—a branch that started several generations ago with Josiah Gaines, the son of Caroline Jane Hargrove and Willie Gaines. Would the Gaines family, well established in San Antonio years ago, take an interest in becoming acquainted with their distant cousins, or in visiting their five-hundred-acre section of the state park being created? I hoped family friendship would develop, and Janet and I had already volunteered to work with Estelle and David on the park project.

People were talking to each other. Estelle and Uncle Cotton were chatting away, probably about the state park, which would have intrigued Uncle Cotton.

I could hear Josh talking with Janet about returning the padlock and rusty chain to the ranch gate where I'd found it. The chain still rattled on the floor of Janet's car.

Someone who looked a lot like Janet introduced herself to me. It was Cousin Miranda, asking for her promised copy of Estelle's documents. I had a package prepared and I gave it to her. Miranda then asked if she could also have copies of the treasure chest letters? And the journal, too? We agreed to get together and go over things soon.

Bob threaded his way through the crowd and joined me. "I've got another question for your Great-Aunt Hettie. Is your Uncle

Cemetery Whites

Henry named after the Henry rifle?"

"Oh, I know the answer to that. His mother's maiden name was Henry; he must have been named for her family."

"Well, that makes sense. That's why there are so many Davids and Toms among the Hargroves in every generation," Bob said.

I could tell he was teasing me, but I didn't say anything back. I smiled at him, and he put his arm around my shoulders. We stood together and waited for the time to go home.

Some people were leaving. They passed by the table with my newspapers and took them along. I'd hear about my articles later; they'd call or e-mail me if they had something to say.

Our drought had broken over the weekend. Rain had poured down over Texas, sweeping down from the northwest. Wildflowers would be plentiful in April, the time of our festival. Tours, visits to all the historic museums, and visits with various relatives filled the calendar.

There were plenty of things to do all spring and summer. The state park project would take Janet and me to San Antonio; I had a new job in journalism; and maybe I'd start writing a book about our family history.

And of course, there was Bob. His special presence in my life was growing.

Bob seemed to know that I was thinking of him. He squeezed my shoulder with his arm and looked down at me.

"Ready to go?" he asked me.

"Any old time," I told him. We gathered our jackets, said our goodbyes, and started our long way home.

© Black Rose Writing

Breinigsville, PA USA
04 March 2011
256955BV00002B/3/P